He appeared in the doorway in nothing but track pants

Annie wished he'd put on a T-shirt at least, so she wouldn't have to look at all that bronzed male nakedness.

"Okay. What do you want to say?"

She sucked in a breath and forced herself to meet his eyes. "I'm pregnant." And, just in case he didn't get it the first time, "I'm having a baby. Your baby. In about seven and a half months."

Silence.

She watched, desperate for some sign, but it was as if Steve had turned to stone—except for his Adam's apple, which bobbed once. His complexion had turned a whiter shade of pale. And his wide-eyed gaze dipped to her waist.

She saw his emotion, held in check by rigid self-control. The tight fists and clenched jaw. And it was impossible to miss the wonder—and the fear—in his eyes.

"Pregnant," he murmured. "Sweet heaven."

ONE NIGHT BABY

When passion leads to pregnancy!

All-consuming attraction...spine-tingling kisses...
unstoppable desire.

With tall, handsome, sexy, gorgeous men like
these, it's easy to get carried away with the
passion of the moment—and end up
unexpectedly, accidentally, shockingly
PREGNANT!

And whether she's his one-night lover,
temporary love slave at work or permanent
mistress, family life hadn't been in his plan—
well, not yet, anyway! The sparks will fly, the
passion will ignite and their whole worlds
will be turned upside down—and that's before
the little bundle of joy has even arrived!

Don't miss any books in this exciting new
miniseries from Harlequin Presents®!

Anne Oliver
PREGNANT BY THE PLAYBOY TYCOON

ONE NIGHT BABY

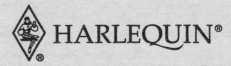

HARLEQUIN®

TORONTO • NEW YORK • LONDON
AMSTERDAM • PARIS • SYDNEY • HAMBURG
STOCKHOLM • ATHENS • TOKYO • MILAN • MADRID
PRAGUE • WARSAW • BUDAPEST • AUCKLAND

Recycling programs
for this product may
not exist in your area.

ISBN-13: 978-0-373-12817-4
ISBN-10:   0-373-12817-7

PREGNANT BY THE PLAYBOY TYCOON

First North American Publication 2009.

Copyright © 2008 by Anne Oliver.

www.eHarlequin.com

Printed in U.S.A.

All about the author...
Anne Oliver

When not teaching or writing, **ANNE OLIVER** loves nothing more than escaping into a book. She keeps a box of tissues handy—her favorite stories are intense, passionate, against-all-odds romances. Eight years ago she began creating her own characters in paranormal and time-travel adventures, before turning to contemporary romance. Other interests include quilting, astronomy, all things Scottish and eating anything she doesn't have to cook. Sharing her characters' journeys with readers all over the world is a privilege...and a dream come true. Anne lives in Adelaide, South Australia, and has two adult children. Visit her Web site at www.anne-oliver.com. She loves to hear from readers. E-mail her at anne@anne-oliver.com.

To family

CHAPTER ONE

STEVE ANDERSON needed sleep. And the last thing he needed after a frustrating day investigating a glitch in a client's security system was his resident night-time fantasy interrupting that sleep.

He scowled at the sporty Honda parked outside the family home he shared with his sister, Cindy, before parking his ute in the garage. Anneliese Duffield, daughter of Melbourne's renowned heart surgeon, Dr Marcus Duffield, had dropped by. Cindy's best friend.

And sleep interrupter extraordinaire.

He passed the late-model silver vehicle on his way inside—an extravagant twenty-first birthday present from her parents—and scowled again, annoyed that he still remembered that evening so well.

They'd barely seen one another in those past three years—Anneliese had been overseas with her parents for eighteen months and he'd been frequently interstate on business. When they had, on the odd occasion, crossed paths, she'd made it blazingly clear she didn't enjoy his company. But he'd seen her laughing and relaxed when she hadn't known he was watching…and there was something about her besides the hot pull of lust. Something that always tied him up in knots…

Stabbing his key in the back door, he reminded himself she

tied everyone up in knots because she didn't possess an ounce of responsibility. Any resulting problems were sorted out by Mum and Dad.

But he could always smell the fragrance she left in the air. French, he imagined, and distinctively unique, as if she'd had it bottled exclusively. And perhaps she had—wouldn't that be just like her? Whatever, it always seemed to lodge in his nostrils and settle beneath his skin like an itch he couldn't scratch.

He could see now that his sister and her friend were engrossed in conversation and cheesecake in the kitchen and oblivious to him. He warned himself he should keep walking, head straight to his room. Take a shower. Something. Anything. Instead, he leaned against the door frame and watched Anneliese.

Sharp cheekbones caught the kitchen light. Deep auburn hair, styled in a blunt chin-length bob, framed an oval face. Curves in all the right places. Perfection.

But it was her eyes that drew him. Not quite green, not quite blue. The colour of blue gums on a misty day. Eyes that could haunt his dreams.

If he let them.

Irritated because on too many occasions to count they'd done just that, he pushed away from the doorway with a brusque, 'Hi.'

Anneliese's head swivelled to face him, eyes wide and wary, which irritated him all over again, but he tried for amiable. 'Can a hungry man get some of that?'

And, yep, no prizes for guessing how she'd interpret that question, he realised as soon as the words left his mouth, because just like that her eyes cooled, her posture stiffened. The spoon slid from her mouth, leaving a smear of cream on her lower lip before he was aware he'd been watching her mouth pout into that little moue of surprise.

Another strike against him.

Unable to resist adding to her discomfort, he tapped his own lip on the corresponding spot, saw the tip of her tongue dart out and lick it off. Her gaze remained locked with his, like a stunned rabbit's.

Cindy, completely oblivious, bounced out of her chair, her dark pony-tail swinging, then reached up to kiss his cheek. 'Of course you can. I was hoping you'd get here before Annie left. I'll get another plate.'

And the view was clear again. Anneliese looked as sweet and innocent as icing on a wedding cake and he struggled against inappropriate images that fuelled his blood further. 'How's it going, Anneliese?'

'Steve…'

She seemed to have trouble articulating his name. Her trademark perfume wafted to his nose like a summer-filled breeze. She was wearing well-tailored dark trousers and a soft-looking striped sweater in the colours of coconut ice. Gold highlights shone through her hair, courtesy of some expensive salon procedure, no doubt.

A flush tinged her cheeks and a frown formed between perfectly arched brows. She seemed to draw herself taller and retreat behind some kind of defence at the same time. 'I better be go—'

'Don't let me interrupt whatever you were discussing. It sounded important.' Steve held Anneliese's eyes a moment longer, wondering what it would be like to break down that wall and—just once—see a smile directed at him that reached those eyes.

'Here you are. Passion-fruit—your favourite.'

'Thanks, sis.' He remained standing as he took the plate Cindy held out to him. Carved off a mouthful of cheesecake from the box on the table with a spoon.

'And it *is* important.' Cindy addressed his comment. 'Annie's insisting on driving all the way to Surfers Paradise on Wednesday—alone—and I'm trying to talk her out of it.'

Steve caught Cindy's concerned look. *Good luck with that.* From what he'd observed, *Annie* always got her own way. But he agreed with his sister—he didn't like the thought of any woman driving across the continent on her own.

He told himself it wasn't his problem, but it didn't quite work. His jaw clenched in aggravation. 'I imagine your father's not keen on you driving halfway across the country alone.'

'I'm twenty-four. Old enough to make my own decisions.'

The cheesecake turned sour in Steve's mouth. Some people were never old enough—make that *mature* enough. Didn't it matter to Anneliese that her mother had died not five weeks ago and her father might need her here? Queensland's Gold Coast was a bustling tourist strip—in his opinion not a place you'd go to contemplate your life or heal the hurts. And she should be doing those things here, with her father, not flitting off inter-state.

He fought the impulse to sneer, scraped his spoon across the bottom of the cake box. 'Some decisions should be made after careful consideration to others' needs.' He schooled his voice to neutral except it didn't come out the way he'd intended.

For a flicker of time he saw something deeper than pain cross those misty eyes, but he didn't have time to ponder because Cindy spoke.

'Steve…' she said quietly, turning into him and touching his arm. 'You know Annie's dealing with serious personal issues right now. She's fragile. Be gentle.'

His gaze slid over Anneliese's curves beneath the soft sweater and his hands curled around the tingle. *Gentle.* He could imagine being gentle with Anneliese a little too vividly.

Cindy patted at his arm again. 'I know you're flying to Brisbane in the next week or two for work and I've come up with an idea… You've got reliable staff here to cover for you, so if you're not in a hurry you could drive with Annie, look out for her…'

A choked sound bubbled up from Anneliese's throat as he stared at Cindy. He was momentarily speechless. Obviously her friend was, too. *Look out for Anneliese?* As in personal escort? He felt a sinking feeling in the pit of his stomach. Just the two of them. All the way to Queensland. Presumably in her sporty car that was way too confining for his six-foot-plus frame.

Cindy must have intuited his answer because she cajoled and patted some more. 'Please, Steve. I'd go myself but I'm trying out for that promotion and I can't get the time off work.'

He turned to Anneliese, who looked as gobsmacked as he, but aimed his question at Cindy. 'Don't you think you should be asking Anneliese what she has to say?'

'She'll do it for me.' Barely a glance at her friend. 'Won't you, Annie? There. It's done.'

He let out a long slow breath. He must have nodded or something because Cindy smiled up at him, and it seemed the arrangement was final.

'Hey,' she soothed, moving to Anneliese's side and rubbing her back. 'He's my big brother, Annie. The one guy you *can* trust is Steve. He'll look after you. There's no need to worry.'

'I'm not worried.' Anneliese cleared her throat, her eyes reverting to that familiar frigid blue. 'Thanks all the same, but I don't need a passenger cluttering up the journey with unnecessary conversation. Nor do I need someone holding my hand and tucking me into bed at night.'

Steve blinked at the image. 'I'm not the talkative type.' As for the rest... Their eyes met and he could've sworn they were seeing the same image. Two naked bodies sliding over crisp white sheets, her long legs gripping his hips, impatient feminine sighs filling the air...

She averted her eyes, biting down on her bottom lip as the flush in her cheeks spread to her neck.

Stick to the matter at hand, Steve. And Cindy was right. The girl needed a bodyguard. If he didn't offer... Resigned to his fate, he set his plate down. 'I have a few security systems to install up north and some prospective clients to see. If you're worried about space, I travel light. I can send the equipment I need by air to Brisbane and...' He paused at a sudden ruckus emanating from the laundry. 'What the heck is that noise?'

'Fred. My magpie. Cindy's going to babysit him for me while I'm away.' Anneliese tipped up her chin. 'I'm not going to Brisbane. I'm going to Surfers.'

He smiled at her cool disdain. 'My timetable's flexible and Brisbane's only an hour's drive farther on.'

Cindy hugged Anneliese. 'I'd rest so much easier with Steve going, too, and knowing you were in safe hands.'

Steve hitched a shoulder inside his flannel shirt and tucked his 'safe' hands in the back pockets of his jeans.

Anneliese's nostrils flared as she inhaled a deep breath, then she looked at Steve and said, 'Very well. Wednesday. And I want to get an early start. 6:00 a.m.'

He held her gaze, saw doubts and schemes stir in the depths, but he only nodded. 'See you at your place at five forty-five. My mobile number.' Without breaking eye contact, he reached into his pocket and withdrew his business card, set it on the table in front of her: Angel-Shield Security Systems. 'In case there's a change of plan.'

One hand rose to her throat, drawing his attention to the way her breasts rose and fell as if she was having difficulty catching her breath. She pushed up from the table with a mumbled, 'Excuse me...'

Anneliese barely got the words past her lips while her gaze remained locked with Steve's. Her feet stayed glued to the floor for what seemed endless moments before she could unfreeze her brain, order her legs to move and escape to the sanctuary of Cindy's *en suite* bathroom.

Breathless, she leaned back against the door. Her legs still felt weak, her hands clammy as she slid them over the front of her trousers.

Steve Anderson. Her best friend's brother. Worse, the man she tried her utmost to avoid. Why did he have to turn up *right now*?

Since the night of her twenty-first party she'd managed—mostly—to give him a wide berth, which made the memory of the last few moments all the more intense. She blinked, but his image was still there, lounging insolently between her eyes. Six-foot-plus of disarming man in faded black jeans and hiking boots.

He had hair the colour of teak and permanently in need of a trim, dark eyes, tanned skin. Still wearing his old padded vest—a sleeveless, shapeless black thing with a red logo of some car manufacturer or other on the back.

Did he ever take it off? No. She didn't want to think about him taking it off. Because then she'd start thinking about that soft flannel shirt beneath and how it would feel if she touched it. Touched him. Right there in that V of flesh where a few masculine hairs curled over the collar.

She bit back a moan, moved to the basin and wrenched on the tap, letting the cold water flow over her hands. She'd rather die before she succumbed to that temptation. When she needed a partner for social occasions the men she associated with treated her with respect, dropping her home with a chaste kiss at the door. As she expected. As she preferred, she reminded herself.

Steve Anderson wouldn't stop at the chaste kiss. Or the front door.

She had an even more disturbing feeling that she wouldn't try to stop him either.

He was…dangerous.

His deep voice vibrated all the way up the passage and through the bathroom door. She heard Cindy's laugh, then…silence. She breathed a sigh of relief.

She flicked water over her neck and checked her hair but avoided looking too closely at her face, afraid of what she'd see—tell-tale flushed cheeks and too-wide eyes that would confirm what she'd spent more than the past three years denying: for some inexplicable reason Steve Anderson called to her on some primal level. Inexplicable because why she'd be attracted to someone who changed women as often as he changed underwear, she didn't have a clue.

So she had no intention of letting him accompany her halfway across the country. She was leaving Tuesday. Tomorrow. Staying one day ahead. 'Sorry, Cindy,' she murmured. 'I don't care how trustworthy you think your brother is, or how concerned you are for me.'

Discovering the real Anneliese, taking charge of her life was something she needed to do alone. Avoiding hot-looking men that unbalanced her equilibrium while she searched was another.

Only a few stars pricked a sky heavy with clouds as Anneliese loaded the last bag into her car early Tuesday morning and closed the rear door on the hatchback.

'Bunnykins.'

She turned at the familiar name, her heart aching at the sight of her father in his striped pyjamas framed by the light spilling from the hallway onto the veranda. His greying hair stood up in spikes, his breath fogged the crisp pre-dawn air.

'Daddy, it's freezing and you haven't got your dressing gown on. Go back inside. I told you last night I wouldn't leave without saying goodbye. Go on, Dad,' she said gently. 'I'll be there in a minute.' As she watched him shuffle back inside guilt flooded her and she considered forgetting the whole thing. Until five weeks ago her life had been on track, her world safe and secure. She could never have imagined leaving the sanctuary of her parents' love and the only home she'd ever known to travel seventeen hundred kilometres to a remote place she'd never seen.

But that safe, secure world had crashed.

Her whole life had been a lie.

Her parents, the two people she'd trusted, who'd taught her that truth was gold, had lied to her. Betrayed her. Lying by omission was still a lie. She owed it to herself to uncover it all before she talked to her father.

She found him in the kitchen emptying the teapot to make a cup of tea. 'Let me do that.' Taking the pot from his hands, she opened the tea caddy and dumped in two scoops of leaves. 'Remember, I've cooked up a dozen meals. They're labelled and in the freezer for you. I've done all the ironing and stocked the pantry.'

'Your mother would be so...' He trailed off, spreading his hands.

'Don't, Daddy.' Tears pricked at her eyes, hot points of pain. Snuggling against his chest, she curled into his warmth and familiarity one last time. She'd have done anything to spare him pain, but she was hurting, too. Hurting because she couldn't yet tell him the truth about why she had to leave. Aching because that made her as guilty as he. But she had to do what she had to do, and it had to be now.

'When I come back, we'll talk.' She straightened. 'I have to go now to beat the traffic. I'll be careful, Daddy. I'll be okay.'

'I know you will, Annie.'

He sounded more convinced than she was herself, and she breathed a sigh of partial relief in his confidence and kissed his cheek. *I love you* hovered on her tongue, but somehow she couldn't bring herself to say the words that had always come so easily.

He squeezed her arms, stepped back.

She picked up her handbag, then walked through the house, not allowing herself even a glimpse of the antique furniture and the porcelain art pieces in the formal lounge, the crystal chandelier gracing the entrance hall. Not even her mother's straw gardening hat on the stand by the front door. Especially not her hat—one of the few items Anneliese hadn't been able to remove when clearing out her mother's things.

She climbed into her car, took a breath as she set the vehicle into motion, pressing the remote to open the gate as she followed the curved lawn-edged drive.

Could she really do this? All those kilometres. All by herself. She'd never had to be independent. But she'd wanted to be— *needed* to be—and she was starting right now. Her heart sat like a lead ball in her chest, but she tightened her grip on the steering wheel and focused on the view ahead.

That was when she saw the figure of a man in the middle of the driveway as the gates swung open. Her headlights caught the glint of dark hair, the outline of long muscled denim-clad legs, brown eyes...and that familiar black vest. He smiled and his teeth gleamed in the light's beam as he bent down and swung a backpack over one shoulder.

Oh, no. Her breath catching, she hit the brakes. He set his hands on the bonnet of her car. Strong and tanned and big, and she had the weirdest sensation that Steve Anderson wasn't putting those hands on the curves of her car so much as laying claim to her body.

CHAPTER TWO

STEVE had the passenger door open and was tossing his bag in the back before Anneliese could lower her window to tell him to get out of her way. Scooping her jacket and handbag off the seat before she could think about where the accelerator was, or remember to lock the passenger door.

'Good morning, Anneliese.' Grinning at her, he checked his watch. 'Right on time. Two minutes past six. I like a woman who's punctual.'

'It's *Tuesday*.'

He smelled of the wind, damp and male and she knew his jaw would feel cold and bristly against her palm if she slapped it right now as she wanted to. Or if she curled her fingers around it and simply felt.

When he didn't reply, she gritted her teeth. 'We were leaving on Wednesday.'

'But you changed the schedule, I see.' With that grin still in place, he hauled the seat belt over his shoulder. 'Well, then, let's get going—we want to beat the rush hour. Or are you waiting for me to drive?'

'Oh, no. You are *not* getting your hands on this baby.' She blew out a breath, super aware of the silence and his gaze on her, as if he were asking whether she was referring to her car or her person. *Both*, she thought, pressing the remote to close the gates behind her.

He didn't speak again, which gave her time to get her brain into gear. And perhaps it was better this way. She wasn't alone any more. Already her anxiety had slipped a notch. If he kept to his side of the car and didn't talk to her in that sexy deep voice, she could handle it. If nothing else, Steve Anderson's presence alone would divert her focus away from all she was leaving behind.

She told herself she was calm, calm, calm. But she accelerated, turning into the road with a screech of tyres on bitumen, and felt the sudden movement as he gripped his seat belt. 'And no handy hints on how to drive.'

A few moments of silence prevailed. 'Just an observation...' he ventured. 'We should've turned right at the last intersection if you want to get onto the interstate before lunch.'

And she realised the waver in his voice was more of a vibration. *Of amusement*. 'Habit,' she muttered, checking her rear-vision mirror and furious with herself for allowing him to make her forget. She turned off, then doubled back.

'I imagine it is,' he drawled. 'All those exclusive Toorak Road boutiques just down the way.' She felt his gaze slide over her lemon silk blouse and grey light wool trousers. There was probably a sneer somewhere in there, but it was hard to tell because she was so engrossed with the sound of his deep voice rumbling in his chest.

'*The way* to my father's consulting rooms,' she corrected icily. 'Where I *work*.' And desperately switched the conversation to him. 'I imagine this trip is seriously impinging on your social life.'

'Not at all,' he said comfortably.

Was he between relationships, then? Did he even do relationships, or were they all one-night stands? She felt her face heat and changed topics fast. 'So you camped outside my house all night?'

'Heck, no. But I had this gut feeling you might change your mind about the day and forget to call me. Weird, huh?'

Her cheeks heated further and she was grateful for the semi-darkness. One hand crept to fiddle with the top button of her blouse, and she wished she could flick it undone to cool the sudden hike in air temperature.

Sweat sprang to her palms and she kept her eyes on the rear lights of the car in front. She could try turning down the car's heating, but that would be like admitting he'd made her hot. Which wouldn't have happened if she was alone.

'Except you didn't forget, did you?' he continued in that rumbly voice. 'You had no intention of calling me.'

'I already told you, I don't need a passenger. You could travel at your own speed and convenience. Fly like most business people. It's not too late. I can—'

'Maybe I don't need a driving partner either.' He cut her off, his tone sharp, all trace of humour gone. 'Have you considered that maybe I only agreed to this because I want to put Cindy's mind at rest, not to mention your father's?'

Guilt stabbed at Anneliese. She'd been so caught up in her own problems she hadn't given Cindy a thought.

They came to a snarl in the traffic and she slowed to a stop. 'Okay,' she conceded. 'You're right, I'm sorry. Perhaps you should call her. Tell her not to worry, big brother's got everything under control.'

'Too early yet. But I sent her a text before you opened the gate.' The humour seemed to be back in his voice as he stretched his arms and rolled his shoulders.

She tapped her fingers on the steering wheel and steeled herself to look at him. 'So sure of yourself, aren't you?'

He nodded. 'Pretty much. Whereas you...' He turned to

her. 'You're not—never have been. Your face is an open book. A very pretty book, but open nonetheless.'

His look was so potent, so *knowing* she wanted to shrivel up and die of embarrassment. Because he was right. Instead of the mask she usually retreated behind, anger bubbled up and she stared right back. 'Maybe I wanted you to read the message that said: I don't want you with me.'

'True,' he said slowly. 'But then I'd have to ask myself why that is.' His gaze dipped to her mouth, a glide of sensation as if his fingers were tracing the outline and texture.

A tingle danced down her spine. How would his fingers feel against her lips? Warm or cool? Light and gentle or rough and sure? Would they feel the same on other parts of her body? *No.* She tipped up her chin. 'Let me fill you in on why. You're arrogant and intimidating and…earthy.'

Oh, Lord, had she really voiced that last thought aloud? The corner of his mouth twitched. Yep, she'd said it.

'Not the suave and sophisticated type you're used to, Anneliese?'

'That's not what I meant.' She refused to think about the *earthy* dream she'd had last night involving heat and hands and lots of body lotion. And Steve… 'I don't want company because I have a personal and *private* matter to take care of,' she snapped, flushed and furious that they were having this conversation but unable to look away. It was as if he held her gaze with some sort of magnetic force.

'I'm only your travelling companion,' he said without taking his eyes off her. 'Traffic's moving.'

'I'm aware of that.' Jolting out of her semi-trance state, Anneliese returned her attention to the road. From the corner of her eye she saw him settle back in his seat as she inched the car forward again and said, 'I don't need your conversation taking my focus away from my driving.' She didn't need his conversation, period. The road cleared and she planted her foot on the accelerator.

'By all means, focus away.' He crossed his arms. 'And we're not trying to break any world speed records here. You might want to ease your dad's worry and let him know I'm along for the ride.'

Who was he to remind her of her responsibilities? Anneliese took a deep breath. Counted to three, let it out slowly, then said, 'I intend to, as soon as we stop. Have you forgotten it's dangerous, not to mention illegal, to use the phone while behind the wheel?'

'No. Speaking of dangerous and illegal...do you always travel at this speed?'

'When I'm under pressure, yes.'

And no doubt Daddy paid her fines as well. Barely turning his head, Steve studied her covertly. What he was imagining doing to her right now was definitely dangerous, and no doubt illegal, too. But those neat little buttons on her prim little blouse begged to be popped. All the way to her navel. And when he'd eased down her bra and finished exploring her delectable body, he'd just bet that navel was as neat and prim as the rest of her...

He closed his eyes. *Quit now. She's just your travelling companion.*

Not by choice, he reminded himself, for either of them.

And she didn't know it yet, but what she got up to when they arrived in Surfers Paradise was *still* his business. For the sake of Cindy and Marcus and the fact that Steve didn't trust her not to get into trouble he'd just made it his business.

Her perfume wafted beneath his nose and he felt the subtle air movement as she reached over the console to turn on a CD.

Clean, crisp classical violin.

He groaned inwardly. He might have guessed. This did not bode well for a long trip. Feeling constricted, tight, *trapped*, he yanked the zipper of his vest down. Yep. A very long trip.

When he opened his eyes again the music was still classical but she'd turned the volume down and the landscape had changed from suburban to rural. Farming and grape-growing land. Rubbing his eyes, he checked his watch and their speed. If his estimation was correct they were somewhere in the Goulburn Valley. Signs of a town in the distance stirred his hunger. 'Time for breakfast,' he said, stretching out the kinks. 'I'm thinking sausages, hash browns, bacon and eggs washed down with a hot frothy cappuccino.'

'Better make an appointment to see Dad when you get back.'

He turned to look at her to see if she was as serious as she sounded. She'd put on sunglasses so he couldn't be sure. 'I work it off. Don't tell me you're one of those women who skips breakfast.'

'Of course not. But all that oily food… You're hardly going to work it off sitting in a car all day. A balanced—'

'I don't need the lecture.' Obviously she knew it by heart, living with an eminent heart surgeon. 'I'll jog when we stop for the night.'

Tonight. He and Anneliese were going to be sleeping… Close. Disturbing—he might need to lengthen that jog this evening.

'So you like the classics,' he said, more to block out the direction his thoughts were taking than anything else.

'Yes.' Her answer was automatic, her eyes on the road.

'Any other music? Rock and roll?' he asked, hopefully. 'Country and Western? Elvis?' *Heavy metal?*

'We only have classical at home.' A statement, flatly spoken.

'Yeah, but do you like it when you're on your own?'

'Mummy says classical's…' She trailed off, biting her lower lip and blinking rapidly. Swapped the CD in favour of the radio. When the speakers spat out static she turned it off.

Hell. His fault. *Please don't let her cry.* But Steve felt her heartache all the way inside. His own mother hadn't been a part

of his life in for ever. Circumstances might be different—
Marlene Anderson had walked out on her husband and two kids
twenty years ago—but he still remembered the pain. 'Hey…'
he said softly, reaching out to soothe a thumb over her shoulder.

A micro-moment as his fingers skimmed over the skin-
warmed silk, feeling bone beneath flesh, a ridge of bra strap.

A scant second for the jolt of that first contact to rewire his
brain.

He pulled away at the same instant she stiffened and drew
a sharp breath. Well, he decided, curling a fist around the un-
expected heat, that was something to think about. *Or not.*

'It'll heal with time,' he said into the silence, and rather than
look at the rigid woman beside him, he watched the scenery.

The jolt was still vibrating along his bones. *Attraction.* Hell,
he already knew that, but it was more than he'd imagined, and
he'd imagined quite a lot. And different. No other woman had
ever managed to…what? Well, he knew better now—he
wouldn't be so quick to touch her again.

They travelled the rest of the way to the town in silence.

'We'll stop here, then I'll drive for a while,' Steve said as
they cruised down the main street.

Anneliese didn't reply; she seemed to be deep in thought.
She parked outside a bakery and they found a clean laminated
table with the colour scrubbed out of it.

He ordered his big breakfast while Anneliese ordered coffee
and a salad roll. They sat opposite each other to wait for their order.

'You okay?'

Her reply was a tight-lipped, 'Fine, thanks.'

No more than he expected. But she looked fragile, as Cindy
had said. And it wasn't just her mother's passing—he saw
more than grief in her eyes. He saw anger and disillusionment
for starters. *Serious personal issues.*

This time he resisted offering her the comfort of touch, but it went against his nurturing nature and left him feeling inadequate and hollow. 'If you want to unload...'

He didn't think she even heard him. When they'd eaten they used the town's public conveniences, then met up back at the car. 'Sure you don't want to stock up on chocolate before we hit the road? Chocolate's a good comfort food.'

'I'm fine.'

'Okay, but don't tell me I told you so when I break open my giant block of Caramello.' He pulled his sunglasses from his vest pocket. 'I'll drive.'

'Uh...wait up...' She bit her lip, hesitated a second, then dropped the keys in his hand and took off up the street again.

He watched her go, her low heels clicking on the footpath while his thumb stroked over her keys still warm from her hand. She was compact, he thought, eyeing her cute bottom in those hip-hugging trousers and that demure blouse he couldn't seem to stop fantasising about. Neat.

And all zippered up like her expensive gold chain-mesh key-holder.

Scowling, he unzipped it, unlocked the door and yanked it open. He was used to girls who were open, flirtatious, and knew how to have fun. Girls who understood the ground rules: nothing serious. When it wasn't fun any more, for either party, it was time to move on. A girl like Anneliese wouldn't know fun if it laid her on her back and tickled her tummy.

And why he'd come up with that analogy was beyond his comprehension.

A couple of minutes later she was back with something in a slim carry bag. Somewhat breathless, she slid into the passenger seat. She seemed different. Brighter, lighter, as if she'd shed a little of that load off her shoulders. He couldn't see her eyes behind her sunglasses, but a tiny Mona Lisa smile tipped up the corners of her mouth.

Perhaps he'd been wrong about the tummy tickle. Perhaps she didn't know how to have fun because no one had shown her. A flash of heat zapped through his veins, quickly doused. What in hell was he thinking? No, he was sure the ice-maiden act was reserved for him alone—perhaps with another man...

He jerked his gaze straight ahead and slid the key into the ignition. 'All set?'

'Let's go.'

They drove out of town, heading northeast. The sky was lowering, darkening with threatened rain. The trees tossed in the strengthening wind.

Steve was happy to oblige her earlier request for little conversation. After all, what could they possibly have in common?

Except the intense physical awareness of each other.

Yeah, she was aware of him all right. If she'd shifted any farther left, she'd be out the door.

Not that he was looking.

He didn't need to look to know that her blouse had stretched tighter over her breasts when she'd pushed her hair behind her ears. He couldn't help hearing her soft sighs when she wiggled her bottom to find a more comfortable position. And all the while her fragrance teased his nostrils.

It was like an endurance test.

They stopped for a late lunch, then a major accident and a hailstorm held them up. Darkness fell suddenly, like a wet blanket.

They'd swapped driving duty an hour ago, which gave Steve nothing to do but concentrate on *not* thinking about his proximity to Anneliese. The radio had dropped out fifty kilometres back and the silence inside the car was beginning to grate on Steve's nerves. It was past 10:00 p.m. 'We've got to stop somewhere tonight,' he said. 'Any ideas?'

'Ah...I...was hoping we could drive straight through—'

'Nope.' He'd expected that. 'I need a few hours of horizontal.'

'Take a nap now, then. I'm right for a while.' Without taking her eyes off the road, she set the open map on his lap.

He'd hardly closed his eyes when he woke feeling vaguely disoriented. He checked his watch. One hour. Something wasn't right.

She caught his glance and her frown mirrored his. 'I expected we would've been near Moree by now... I think maybe we took a wrong turn somewhere...'

'*We?*'

'I thought—'

'The general condition of this road gave you no clue?' He gestured at the view beyond the windscreen, switched on the car's interior light. 'Why didn't you wake me? Pull over to the side of the road.'

She complied without a word.

'This is where we're headed—*were* headed...' Taking the map from his knee, she spread it out on the dashboard.

'Anneliese. No.' He remained calm—*was* calm, he told himself—as he reorientated the map ninety degrees, pointed to their route. So it was true what they said about women and maps. 'I'll drive.'

'No.' She set the car into gear, turned and headed back the way they'd come. 'What's that noise—?'

'Just what we damn well need—'

They both spoke at the same time.

'Pull over again,' he ordered.

A chill wind wrapped around him as he climbed out. He confirmed the problem, then poked his head inside to give Anneliese the good news. 'We've got a flat.' He zipped his vest as high as it would go. 'Guess we can be thankful it's not something serious or we might be stuck here for hours.'

CHAPTER THREE

A FLAT.

As in tyre.

As in we need the spare.

The spare with the three-month old puncture she'd forgotten about.

Taking a deep breath, Anneliese closed her eyes. A hole seemed to open up in her stomach and she wished she could just crawl into it and disappear. So much for being independent.

'Switch off the engine and help me unload your gear from the boot and I'll change it,' she heard Steve say. 'Maybe we can still make Moree this side of midnight.'

She switched off the car but remained where she was. A muffled 'um' escaped from between her tight lips.

When she opened her eyes she found Steve leaning over the passenger seat, his gaze fixed on hers. 'Tell me you have a jack.'

'I do.'

'Thank heavens for that, then,' he said, backing out again. 'For a moment there, I—'

'But the sparc's…punctured.'

'*The. Spare's. Punctured.*' He enunciated each word as if he needed time to absorb the meaning.

'I never got around to…' she looked away; she didn't think he'd appreciate her bringing into it the fact that Dad considered it a man's job and took care of her car. '…getting it repaired.'

'You planned to drive seventeen hundred k's without having your car checked over first.' She flinched at the sound of a frustrated palm slapping the car's roof. 'I bet you didn't forget your perfume, did you?' He shut the passenger door with a firm thud.

'For your inf…' *Forget it, he can't hear you. He doesn't* want *to hear you.*

And what he'd said was no more than the brutally honest truth.

She watched him in the car's headlights as he walked away, his unkempt hair whipped by the wind. He turned into the glare and motioned her to turn off the lights as he pulled something out of his pocket.

What in heaven's name would she have done if she'd been alone? Exactly what he was doing, she thought, watching him punch numbers into his mobile. But she breathed a sigh of relief that he had everything under control and slumped down in her seat.

Except hadn't she sworn to take control of her own life? She jackknifed up again. Wasn't that why she'd begun this journey? To make changes? Forget that if she'd been responsible he wouldn't be making calls on a lonely road in the middle of the night. Someone else taking charge. Again. Worse, it was Steve, the man she always seemed to fall apart in front of.

She couldn't take her eyes off him. Ratty vest aside, he was…what? She'd never been so aware of any man the way she was aware of Steve. Because he was different? Because he didn't treat her the way her usual dates did?

Her mind spun back to her twenty-first party at an exclu-

sive Melbourne club. Most of the guests had left and he'd
turned up late to collect Cindy and somehow Anneliese had
found herself alone in the car park with Steve...

'Happy birthday, Anneliese.'

His deep-timbred voice resonated along her bones, sending
excitement fizzing through her veins like the celebratory champagne she'd been drinking all night, and she quite simply froze.

'Thank you,' she managed—barcly—mcsmerised by a
smile that was as potent as the intensity of his dark eyes. She'd
have walked past him, but even motionless he seemed to be
blocking her way. Her feet remained glued to the concrete.

His hair stood up in spikes, and that facial fuzz had to be at
least three days old. There was a smear of grease on his arm,
as if he'd been playing mechanic. In tattered jeans and sneakers
and a black T-shirt that looked as if it had been spray-painted
over that mile-wide chest, obviously he didn't care that this
place had a dress code, even if he was only on driving duty.

And yet her pulse took no notice of the fact that this was the
type of man she avoided.

'You look sensational tonight,' he said when she didn't
move. Didn't speak.

Just stood like a statue in her filmy white organza gown,
eyes fused with his while his body heat radiated across the too-
close space between them. 'Thank you again.' She cleared her
throat and attempted to paste a smile on her stiff lips. 'Cindy's
inside.'

'Sorry I'm late—I've been working on her car.' He hesitated
a beat before saying, 'Do I get a birthday kiss?' He must have
presumed she'd comply because he promptly stepped in and
she got a whiff of motor oil and healthy sweat.

Her heart thundered; her breath stalled. Terror invaded her
body. Terror that she'd fall at his feet in a mindless quivering
heap. She flung out a hand in front of her. 'Touch me and

I'll…' She trailed off. Already her lips were tingling, her hand falling limp to her side, her body swaying towards him.

Her numbed brain registered a flicker of hurt behind the heat in his gaze. 'And you'll…what, Anneliese?'

She could feel the vibration of his lips, his breath, in the air between them and closed her eyes for the final assault.

Then…nothing.

'No. On second thoughts, I don't think so,' he murmured. 'You'd just spend the rest of the night awake and restless and wishing for more than just a kiss.'

She gasped as her eyes snapped open. His mouth was still a whisper away from hers. But not close enough.

Never going to be close enough.

Her cheeks stung with humiliation while her hands itched to slap that arrogant smile off his face. And her lips still ached.

Straightening, he stepped away. 'And you'd hate yourself in the morning…'

Anneliese relived the emotions as she watched him through the windscreen. On the few occasions they'd run into each other, neither of them had mentioned that evening again. But it was always there, a silent wall between them.

So of course he hadn't invited himself on this trip. He'd done it for Cindy's peace of mind, and her father's. She watched him rake a hand through his over-long hair and promptly dismissed the image of that hand touching her with the same wild abandon.

He looked thoroughly untamed right now with the wind flapping against his vest and the threadbare patches in the knees of his jeans. Some women went for that look. A lot of women apparently. A disconcerting blip interrupted her pulse… That was how she knew it wouldn't be a chaste kiss at the front door.

As for her birthday non-kiss… Well, she'd never know.

He turned and headed back to the car and even in the night's dimness she didn't miss the impatient snap in his long strides, the grim face as he shoved the mobile in his jeans pocket. Chill air bowled into the car, sweeping away the residual warmth from the car's heating as he swung the door open and slid inside. He smelled of spice and winter grass and she had to force herself not to gulp it in.

'First off, I apologise,' he clipped. 'That gibe about the perfume was uncalled for.'

She inclined her head. 'You called it as you see it. What now?'

'Can't get a signal.' He closed his eyes briefly, then turned to her, his jaw tight and shadowed with the day's stubble. 'I'll try again later. Unless a car comes by, we're stuck here. And since we'll need a tow, we're here for the night in any case.'

She told herself the tight clench in the region of her stomach was because she hadn't eaten, that the only reason her skin prickled was because she was cold. But it was more than that. Her irresponsibility had got them into this mess. And now they were stranded. Together. Close together. 'I'm sorry.'

'These things happen.' He squeezed her shoulder in a totally non-sexual way and his expression relaxed a little, but warmth spiralled from his touch down to her fingertips.

She'd just bet *these things* didn't happen to Steve.

He blew on his hands. 'Do you have a rug, or something we can share while we wait?'

Share body heat with Steve Anderson? Her pulse accelerated and her skin prickled anew and she shivered involuntarily. For a moment she considered saying no, but that was about as dumb as travelling without an inflated spare tyre.

'There's a quilt in the boot.' Scrambling out, she hugged herself against the wind as she headed to the back of the car, then began pulling out bags.

Steve appeared at her side, shrugging off his vest. 'Here. You're shivering.' Before she knew what he was about, he'd slung the vest around her shoulders, enveloping her in his spicy warmth.

She didn't need it. She didn't need to feel the slippery sensation of the lining against her breasts through her jumper, didn't want to be surrounded by his masculine scent. 'No... I'm okay.'

Irritation and impatience sparked in his eyes as she looked up at him. 'Keep it, I don't feel the cold,' he said, pulling the quilt out. 'Get back in the car, I'll finish up here.'

She did as he requested, dragging her arms through the openings in the vest on the way. Steve joined her a couple of minutes later with the quilt—her *bedroom* quilt with the extra down filling that seemed to shrink the limited space even further.

'Slide your seat back.' His breath tickled her ear and his hands looked big and dark and masculine on the familiar pink floral fabric as he adjusted it over them both.

Whoa. Her whole body went rigid; her heart stalled. It was like being in bed with him. She only had to lean a little more to the left to find out how his lips would feel against hers, and she was tempted. She'd never acted out anything like that in her life.

'The steering wheel's going to get in your way,' he said patiently. 'And if we want to maximise the quilt's effectiveness we need to be close.'

'Close?' she repeated, her eyes drifting to his mouth again. Her voice came out as a whisper.

Then she realised he was waiting for her to oblige with the seat. She slid it back a couple of notches so that they were shoulder to shoulder. His heat burned through her jumper where they touched. Only the handbrake prevented their thighs from abrading. Thank heavens. She remained rod-stiff, closed her eyes and counted. One, two—

'I won't hurt you, Anneliese.'

The tenderness and absolute sincerity in his voice slid over her like the finest silk on polished wood. 'I know that. You're Cindy's brother.'

A pause while he shifted—probably to a different angle—bumping her shoulder, but she wasn't looking, so she didn't know. Except…she could feel his gaze on her face, could hear the slow rise and fall of his breathing.

'Do you only ever see me as Cindy's brother?' he said into the silence.

Oh, not a fair question. 'Since I only see you when I'm with Cindy, the answer's yes.'

'Interesting.'

'Isn't that how you see me? As Cindy's friend?' She opened her eyes to find herself looking into direct and piercing eyes, his normally amber gaze coal-dark in the dimness, and swallowed.

'We're not with Cindy now.'

Anneliese's heart stumbled against her ribcage and she looked away, into the night. *That* was his answer?

Whatever it was—a mistake, a slip of the tongue, an accusation—seemed to snap his patience. He shifted abruptly and his tone changed yet again. 'I often wonder how it is that the two of you hit it off so well.'

Her gaze swung back to him. 'I often wonder how you two can be brother and sister.'

He smiled. And, oh…my… The corners of his eyes crinkled, his mouth tipped up boyishly, revealing an endearingly crooked tooth. She'd never noticed that before, she thought hazily. Something stirred along her skin, fluttered in her breast, and she found herself smiling back.

'I've wondered the same thing myself.' He shook his head, warmth and affection for Cindy radiating from those twinkling eyes. 'Maybe I was adopted.'

Anneliese's smile froze. Her veins turned to ice. The almost relaxed warmth she'd been enjoying seeped away, leaving her chilled to the bone. She was elbow-jostling and knee-bumping and breathing the same air with another human being, yet she'd never felt so desolate.

'Hey. What's wrong?' His own smile faded, his eyes narrowed and he reached out, touched a finger to her cheek.

The sensation of being touched, of normal human contact, tempered the pain of the past moment, but she stiffened and drew back, afraid of her own unstable emotions. Afraid of him. His heat, his proximity, his potent and unfamiliar brand of masculinity.

She didn't want Steve getting in the way of what she had to do. She didn't want Steve, period. She just wanted to reach her destination.

'Nothing's wrong. My stomach's talking to me,' she lied, patting her middle. 'In fact it's howling.' She summoned up a casual demeanour and voice to match. 'I'm going to have to admit you were right and beg a couple of squares of that chocolate you so prudently purchased this morning.'

He studied her as if trying to read meaning into her sudden turnabouts of the past few moments, then his mouth quirked and he said, 'You mean that calorie-laden one with the delicious caramel filling? All we've got to eat between us until mid-morning at least?'

She bit her lip, her mouth already watering as she suddenly realised she *was* hungry. 'Yes. I have a half a bottle of water. I'm willing to share if you are.'

'Deal.' He switched on the interior light, opened the glovebox and withdrew a well-depleted block. 'Let's see.' He peeled back the wrapping. 'Six squares. That's two now, one each for breakf—'

'Only six?' She stared at him, incredulous. 'How many were there?'

'A lot more,' he said with a rueful shake of his head. 'I'm afraid chocolate's my number one indulgence.' He broke off a couple of squares, lifted them to her lips with a grin. 'Shall we indulge together?'

Her mouth dropped open in shock and suddenly the air was thick with all the possibilities *that* conjured. The image smouldered in her brain and took hold. She just had to reach out to slip her hand inside the open neck of that disreputable shirt. To pop the top button and climb on top of him and lay her caramel-coated tongue along his collar-bone while he returned the favour with his hands. Inside her blouse, beneath her bra, then— No!

Panic-stricken, her eyes shot to his. The heated gleam in his dark gaze told her all she *didn't* need to know—shared fantasy. Her nipples hardened, the pulse in her neck beat double time. Without thought, she ran her tongue around dry lips, drawing his gaze to her mouth. 'You said one square each…' It was a sultry voice she'd never heard before coming out of her mouth. 'That's two.'

'It's too soft to break further without making a mess.' His voice was deeper, too, as he touched the chocolate to her lips. 'Bite off your half.'

She did as he asked and couldn't control the murmur of delight as the smooth creamy texture flowed over her tongue. Then she saw him pop the remainder into his mouth. His eyelids dipped and she heard his low growl of approval as he savoured the experience. The same way he might when being worked over by a lover…

Heat spread through her body and her mouth went dry. She

swallowed, barely managed to say 'water?' as she withdrew the depleted bottle from the door's pocket.

'After you.'

She unscrewed the top, downed a self-conscious mouthful while he watched. Sucked in a breath while he watched her wipe the moisture from her lips with her fingers. She handed the bottle to him, careful to avoid contact because right now sparks were a high—and dangerous—possibility.

It was almost a relief when they'd both finished, he'd switched off the light and they'd settled an arm's space apart beneath the quilt's warmth in the semi-darkness. She couldn't help the sigh that escaped.

'Are you tired?' Steve asked. 'You can nap—I'll keep watch.'

Yes, she was. But she doubted she could sleep even if she wanted to, and no way was she going to let herself succumb to unconsciousness with Steve watching. 'I'm fine.' Though it might be preferable to this silent awareness that surrounded them. Outside the wind whistled around the car, leaves swirled along the rough road, but inside their shared warmth beneath the quilt created an intimacy that bordered on pain.

'Okay. So, I've admitted mine—what's your weakness, Anneliese?'

His question caught her unawares and took her a moment to think past the first thought that flared in her mind—*you*—which was crazy, and not one she wanted to think about. Especially now, if ever.

'Red shoes,' she said finally. 'And teddies…ah…not to be confused with underwear… I mean the soft furry abandoned kind. You know.'

A knowledgeable *experienced* smile played around his mouth. 'I do.'

'Yes. Well.' She swallowed. 'I can't go past a second-hand

or antique shop without checking if there's one lying in a box somewhere wondering why they were abandoned...'

Her voice broke and she gazed at the windswept vista beyond the windows. *Not* something Steve Anderson needed to know about. With a deliberate throat-clearing, she brightened her voice, attempted a smile and turned to him. 'I have sixty-seven at the last count.'

His brows rose. 'Shoes or teddies?'

'Teddies. You don't count your shoes—that'd take all the enjoyment out of shopping for more.'

'Shopping,' he murmured, with something like contempt and the heat she'd seen in his eyes moments ago cooled. She could read his expression, could almost hear the words forming in his mind. *Spoiled rich chick.*

'It's a girl thing,' she said in her defence. 'You wouldn't understand.'

'Here's something I don't understand,' he said slowly with that same remote detachment. 'Tell me why Dr Marcus Duffield's only daughter is so set on leaving her father when he needs her most and driving to Surfers Paradise.'

Anneliese swallowed over the ball of pain that lodged in her chest, expanded and crept up her throat. She curled her fingernails into her palms till she was sure they'd draw blood to stop herself from the urge to slice into him the way he'd so neatly and precisely sliced into her. 'That's none of your business.'

'I called on your dad last week. Apart from the grieving process, he's worried about you, and I don't think his own health's a hundred per cent.'

'I'm—'

'He doesn't need the added stress and it concerns me.' He steamrolled ahead. 'He gave Dad a new life. He'd still be alive if not for the accident.' His voice remained low-pitched and reasonable. 'Marcus doesn't deserve what you're doing.'

Steve the expert, laying the guilt at her feet with exasperating calm. 'So you're an authority on other people's family business now?' She shook her head, the tears she'd been fighting blurring her vision. 'You know nothing about it.'

'Then tell me. Explain why you're so obsessed about inanimate objects like stuffed toys and shoes when you should be directing your concern towards your father at this time.'

'Because my mother left me, that's why!' The anguished words left her lips before she could call them back.

'Your mother passed away, Anneliese, she didn't—'

'Stop!' Slamming a fist on her knee, she bit down hard on her lip, furious with herself for the momentary lapse. But the truth was out there: Patricia Duffield *wasn't* her mother. For twenty-four years Anneliese had been lied to. Kept in the dark. Cheated. Pain hammered through her veins with every beat of her heart.

Suddenly the air inside the car was thick, confining. She wrenched open the door.

She wasn't Anneliese Duffield.

Her birth name was Hayley Green and she was adopted.

CHAPTER FOUR

'ANNELIESE…' Steve reached for her but she was already out of the car, yanking off his vest. She left it where it dropped and began running.

He cursed himself as he watched her. But as he reached for the door, he held back, fingers tightening on the handle. Give her a moment.

His eyes narrowed but remained glued to her receding figure. Perhaps he shouldn't have gone so hard on her; she was obviously distressed. His fault, damn it. The instinctive urge to offer support overrode other concerns—such as her anticipated resistance to him.

He climbed out, retrieved his vest from the road and started after her. 'Anneliese, wait!'

She picked up pace at the sound of his voice; he saw her ankle crumple in those damn impractical shoes. 'Leave me alone,' he heard her snap. He couldn't see her face so he couldn't read her expression, but he heard the struggle, the dismay behind the steel in her voice.

'No.' He reached her in less than thirty seconds, felt the tension tremble through her as he turned her around. Her eyes, wide moist pools, looked up at him, vulnerable yet defiant, momentarily stirring emotions he reserved only for his sister. The chill night breeze lifted her hair, bringing her fragrance to his nose.

'Here.' He laid his vest around her shoulders. Again.

She shrugged at it, at him. 'I told you to leave me al—'

'And I said no.' He held the vest firm but not too firm, his hands easily gripping her slim shoulders. 'Not until I know you're all right.'

'Of course I'm not all right. You!' She pushed at him, self-disgust colouring her voice. 'You make me say things I'd never say in my right mind.'

He couldn't help the smile that tugged at his lips as he said, 'There's your answer, then.' He tugged the zip on his vest up, taking care not to notice as his fingers brushed the swell of her breasts. 'And I'm not leaving you alone till you *are* all right.'

He waited till the fight drained out of her, then drew her shivering body against his. Her warmth curved into him, her sigh drifted across his neck. He didn't know what to say so he waited and said nothing while the trees whispered and something scuffled in the roadside vegetation.

Only Anneliese would see her mother's death as some sort of betrayal. Something that hadn't gone her way for once. But she was hurting, and bringing all the emotion to the surface was his fault.

'Come back to the car,' he said to the top of her head.

She leaned back a fraction and looked up at him, her face pale and shadowed with fatigue. A strand of her hair blew across her face and caught against her lips.

Catching the silky strands, robbed of their glorious colour in the night's light, he rubbed them between thumb and forefinger before smoothing them back into place behind her ear. He left his hand there, wanting to feel her skin against his palm. Wanting to tell her everything would be all right. That he was here.

So it seemed natural to lean down and touch his lips to hers. To reassure, to soothe. But as he skimmed her mouth and tasted the tears she hadn't allowed him to see and the sweetness that bloomed through the salt he wasn't reassured. Or soothed.

Beyond the casual flirtations, the odd romantic weekend getaway, he didn't get involved with women. He didn't allow himself to be suckered into their problems or their plans. Not any more. He'd learned the hard way.

But somehow his arms were around Anneliese and hers were on his chest and she was kissing him back, and not getting involved was history. There was an urgency in the way she grabbed fistfuls of shirt and clung. A passion fuelled by anger and hurt and heaven knew what else.

His own passion flared, fuelled not by anger, but by the sensation of her body as it moved up against his, and those little buttons on her blouse... It sparked along his veins as he urged her mouth to give a little, an enticing hint to the secrets within. The taste of caramel, her own rich texture as his tongue slid briefly against hers.

She released his shirt to spread her hands over his chest, every fingertip touching. Tantalising. Then something changed. Her lips remained locked with his but she pushed at him as if she were engaged in some sort of war with herself.

His arms tightened around her a moment more before he willed them to go slack. If only other body parts would follow suit as easily. He remained perfectly still, giving her the option to pull away when she chose. Perfectly still, because any movement was likely to cause pain or embarrassment, or both, and this was about her, not him.

She pulled back, pressing her lips together as if to deny what they'd done, but even the night's shadows couldn't dim the heat of their brief but passionate encounter in her eyes. 'Why did you kiss me? I'm not one of your... I'm not your kind of woman.'

No, she wasn't, but the way she'd responded had left him breathless. 'It wasn't a one-way street, Anneliese. You kissed me, too.'

She took another step back, hugging his vest around her, and if it had been daylight he knew he'd have seen the blush on her cheeks. Then, to his surprise, she looked down and made a point of staring at the bulge in his jeans. 'What were you going to do? Lay me down on the road and do it?'

Her graphic accusation stunned him. Even if his imagination had run away on its own course. 'I can't control my body's response,' he said tightly. 'You're an attractive woman. If you think I'd take advantage of your distress you don't know me at all.'

'I don't. Know you. Except as Cindy's brother.'

'Ah, yes.' And *that* was beginning to annoy him. 'Because you make a habit of disappearing whenever I come home.'

'That's not true.' But they both knew it was. It was there in her gaze as they eyed one another. She cleared her throat. 'I apologise, I shouldn't have said that.'

Yeah, he thought, it cost her to say that. 'Accepted.'

'Even if it was true.'

With the evidence in his jeans what could he say that he hadn't already said? He shrugged, looking away to the low hills in the distance, freeing himself from the spell her eyes seemed to cast over him. 'So we shared a kiss—no big deal—don't beat yourself up over it. In fact, forget it, if it makes you feel any better.'

'I already have. It never happened.' *Liar*, Anneliese admitted to herself, her lips still throbbing with Steve's taste. His scent was imprinted on her brain.

That single solitary kiss would keep her awake and edgy for the next century. Just as he'd said three years ago: *You'd just spend the rest of the night awake and restless and wishing for more than just a kiss.* Oh, she remembered, word for word. Worse, Steve knew it. She knew he knew it.

'I'm going back to the car. It's freezing out here. Are you coming?' He turned around and began walking.

Anneliese watched him stride away, his shirt flapping in the wind. He hadn't even checked to see if she was following. How could he be so casual when they'd just shared such a mind-blowing kiss?

Except that was the kind of man he was; he probably *had* forgotten about it. So she did *not* want to be some place alone and relive it, she was *not* going to think about Steve *that way* at all.

'Chocolate.' He broke the last four squares in half—without crushing them—and offered her two. They were back in the relative warmth and comfort of the car. Steve had taken the driver's side, leaving Anneliese with the edge of the quilt that still held a hint of his residual heat, the lingering scent of his aftershave—not good for her decision not to think about him.

'I thought that was breakfast,' she murmured.

'Take my share—I've had more than enough today. Comfort food,' he reminded her when she made no move to take it.

She nodded, appreciating the simple gesture since there was nothing else till they found a roadhouse, wherever and whenever that might be, and held out her cupped hand. 'Thank you.'

'Okay,' he said slowly, when she'd finished. 'Have you discussed how you feel about your mum with your dad?'

Dad. The memory of him standing on the veranda this morning, looking smaller, frail, as if he'd shrunk somehow. Dad. The man who saved lives, the man who'd given her every opportunity to experience her own life to its fullest. The father who loved her.

The father who'd lied to her.

Not her father.

'No.'

'Don't you think you should have?'

'It's personal. Besides, what would that do to his stress levels?'

He looked at her, his gaze incredulous. 'You're going to Surfers Paradise—alone—you don't think that's adding to it?'

She sucked in a lungful of air. Her sister lived there. Her biological sister. She'd had a sibling for twenty-four years and had no idea what she looked like, who she was as a person. And, no, she wasn't going to open up to Steve, no matter how badly she wanted to unburden her secret. Especially not to Steve. She didn't want to be any more vulnerable to him than she already was.

'You're not pregnant, are you?' His tight voice dragged her back, and she looked into a pair of razor-sharp eyes. Eyes that held definite traces of anger, bitterness and old hurt.

A half-laugh bubbled up, then sobered. Did he have a child out there somewhere from one of his affairs, someone he wondered about? 'Not that it's any of your business but, no, I'm not pregnant and I wouldn't be careless enough to get myself in that situation. There are enough unwanted kids out there,' she finished with her own bitter thoughts of the mother who hadn't loved her enough to keep her.

Her life was in such turmoil, how could she bring another life into the world and give it the happiness it deserved? But if she was... Oh, to have someone that came from your own flesh. To belong. And she was travelling halfway across Australia to find that blood connection. Yet she hadn't replied to the woman called Abigail Seymour she'd found on the Internet adoption site and who worked in a boutique hotel in Surfers Paradise.

And wasn't that the ultimate irony? She couldn't bring herself to take that step. To cross the boundary between Anneliese and a girl called Hayley.

She became aware of Steve's silent scrutiny. And the narrowing of his eyes, the tightness around his mouth. Then he looked past her, his gaze clouded and dark. 'Are you saying a child of yours would be unwanted? That you'd do whatever it took to be rid of the problem?'

'I don't think that's relevant since I'm not pregnant. This trip's important,' she said into the silence. 'It's something I have to do.'

His gaze swung back to her. 'And you've chosen to do it away from any kind of support network. Your father loves you and you're pushing him away.'

At his words, she felt the shivers ripple through her and hugged her arms around her middle, closing her eyes to hide the tears threatening to spill over. 'Butt out of my business, Steve.'

But Steve heard the desperation behind the tough talk and couldn't not touch her. He shifted sideways, slipped his arm around her shoulders…and felt an overpowering need to protect. That protective instinct had cost him his happiness once before, but he didn't let himself think about that now.

For the short time they were here, he cleared his mind of old mistakes and focused instead on Anneliese. On the texture of her hair against his hand, her fragrance, the way she held herself stiff and rigid against his arm. 'Relax. I'm not going to jump you.' But that kiss was still smouldering in his mind…and other parts of his anatomy.

'I know that.' She rolled her shoulders, leaned a little more loosely against his arm, but her voice came out slightly strangled, as if she was only half convinced.

Her head fell back against his arm, exposing her smooth white throat. 'I know how you feel…what you think about me.'

Think? Maybe. Feel—that was a different matter altogether. 'And what do I *think*?'

'That I'm a pampered princess like those rich chicks you see in the media, whining because she isn't above the law when she gets caught drink-driving. Expecting her parents to sort the mess out.' She made a quick jerky movement with her hand. 'And now, just when I'm trying to reclaim some control over my life and be independent and take some responsibility for myself you come along and rob me of that chance.'

'I'm not trying to take anything away from you, Anneliese. Coming with you was Cindy's idea, remember? There's independence and there's independence. And a responsible girl would know the difference.'

'Are you saying I'm irresponsible?'

'No. Not intentionally at any rate.'

'So you *are* saying I'm irresponsible.'

'I don't want to play word games with you.'

But a different kind of game…one involving that delectable mouth currently thinned in vexation and tilted towards him…the one he'd soothed and wanted to explore further, for pleasure this time…

Hell.

Frowning, he peered at his watch. Drummed itchy fingers against the steering wheel. Too many hours to count. He switched on the ignition and fiddled with the radio, trying to get some reception to fill in the time, but all he got was static.

Then Anneliese reached into the passenger door's side pocket and pulled a selection of CDs out of the bag she'd bought earlier in the day. 'Try these.'

He frowned at the covers: one with a collage of street violence and wilderness, another with a humanoid form emerging from the jawlike petals of a metallic rose. '"Urban Plunder" and "Metamorphosis"?'

She met his questioning gaze. 'They were as far away from the classical section as I could get.'

Obviously she had no idea how far. He replaced her violin concerto with 'Metamorphosis'. 'You're a closet heavy-metal fan, then?'

Her brows drew together and she shrugged. 'The covers inspired me.'

'To what, exactly?'

'Make changes.' She flinched as the first track crashed out of the speakers. 'I want to expose myself to new experiences.' But she turned down the volume, leaned back and closed her eyes.

A few moments later she ejected the disc with a murmured, 'It might take time,' and slid in a gentler, middle-of-the-road guitar ensemble.

Not for the first time, as he watched her lashes settle on her cheeks, Steve pondered her life experiences; or more particularly—since her phrase 'exposing herself to new experiences' conjured images he'd be better off not dwelling on—her experiences with the opposite sex.

The way she acted around him—cool, disinterested, flustered even—he wondered if she'd had anything more serious than the odd date. He'd never asked Cindy about Anneliese's love life or lack thereof, because, knowing how girls loved to gossip, he knew his sister would be sure to fill Anneliese in on his casual enquiry and make a big deal of it.

But the way she'd kissed him—as if she couldn't get enough before she'd pushed him away—beneath the ice façade she had an untapped passion just waiting to be tempted out of hiding.

Her head drooped to the right. She was falling asleep, nestling into his armpit like a lover, her hair catching on his stubbled jaw. Her breath warm against his chest. If his arm hadn't been resting behind her neck he'd have got out of this damn car and hit the road a while.

Now he had to sit here, trapped and unwilling to move lest he disturb her while the hard, unwanted heat in his groin spread and throbbed in time with his pulse.

He'd promised Cindy he'd look out for Anneliese and she didn't need to add Steve Anderson to her list of personal problems. He just had to concentrate on the fact that Anneliese was his sister's best friend and everything would be fine.

Anneliese snuggled deeper into the curve of musky warmth beneath her cheek. Steve had abducted her to her parents' garden shed. He'd installed a heavy-duty security system and chained her to the wall where he was doing unspeakable things to her.

Steve… Oh… Please… Don't… She stirred, shifted against his body, aroused, breathless—then opened her eyes and looked straight into those deep-brown all-seeing eyes… *Stop*.

'Morning.' His voice rolled through her, rekindling the fantasy. 'Sleep well?'

She closed her eyes again, rolling her head to shake away images and sensations. 'Fine.' Pressing her lips together against the husky voice issuing from her throat, she pushed upright and away. Shoved the quilt off her shoulders. *Hot, too hot.*

'Must've been some dream.'

'What makes you think I was dreaming?' she clipped, wide awake now and ready to lie through her teeth. 'Did I say something?' And, dear heaven, did she really want to know the answer?

'No.' But there was something in his voice…

She told herself she was better off not knowing and focused her gaze on the rising sun's fiery glint amongst the clouds. 'What time is it?'

'Seven.'

He withdrew his arm from behind her head and rotated his

shoulder, flexed his fingers. Those same long bronzed fingers with their dusting of hair— *No*. She was not going to relive the way they felt as they caressed her from her neck to the backs of her knees and every place in between.

That dream was symbolic of something much deeper. It was clear, so clear now—she'd been smothered all her life, chained to her ageing parents by duty. A security designer expert with his own business, Steve represented those same restrictions. It had nothing to do with Steve, the man.

This was her wake-up call. Her mother's death, the new-found knowledge of her birth and the fact that she had a sister had freed something inside her. Her new direction had already begun—making the decision to embark on this trip, choosing those CDs yesterday—the dream merely confirmed it.

No more chains, no more letting other people govern her life.

CHAPTER FIVE

BY MID-MORNING they'd been towed to the town of Moree near the New South Wales/Queensland border thanks to a passing farmer and were filling up on a very late and very welcome breakfast while the puncture was being repaired.

The waitress, Darlene, a well-stacked blonde in her late thirties, was doing her utmost to tempt Steve into sampling their famous fresh-baked scones. Considering he'd just polished off a mountain-sized Aussie breakfast and double latte, Anneliese didn't fancy Darlene's chances.

Then again, in the short time Anneliese had freshened up in the roadhouse's rest rooms and taken a seat opposite Steve at the worn table setting, she'd learned that Darlene already knew he was single, in the security business and 'just along with his sister's friend for the ride'.

So she wasn't surprised when he told Darlene he'd 'give them a go'. She *was* surprised at her own reaction to the casual flirtation between them. As Steve favoured the waitress with one of those smiles that always sent Anneliese into a spin and watched her saunter off with a sway of her hips, she felt her body turn leaden and the pancakes and maple syrup she'd just splurged on congealed in her stomach. But she didn't have time to think about it because Steve leaned across the table.

'Before you came in Darlene was selling me on Moree's artesian spa baths,' he was saying. 'Hot mineral pools, forty-one glorious degrees. Fancy a dip to dissolve last night's kinks before we hit the road again?' His gaze, when she looked up, was as warm and inviting as the promised dip.

Spooning the froth off her cappuccino, she muttered, 'Did you tell her we're on a strict timetable?' And saw something shift and gel in his expression. 'And I just want to check in, have a shower and sleep for a few hours.'

'She was just doling out the good ole country welcome, Annie.' Smiling suddenly, he leaned forward. 'The same neighbourly charm that barrel-chested farmer offered you when you jumped out of the car and flagged him down this morning.'

'He wasn't flirting with me like all get out.'

'If you didn't notice, either you weren't paying attention or you simply don't know.' He shrugged, sat back again, the smile still in place. 'I wasn't aware we had a timetable. Didn't you say you needed time to think?'

Not in a hot pool. Not with him near-naked and steamy and all that bronzed skin and hard masculine muscle on display. Because that was what she'd be thinking about. She picked up her coffee and stared at the liquid. 'This isn't a holiday—I'll do my thinking when we reach our destination. And don't call me Annie.'

'Cindy calls you Annie,' he pointed out. 'It sounds friendly, and it's easier to say.'

'Cindy *is* my friend.' *And you're not.* Anneliese continued to stare at her coffee rather than look at the man across the table. *You could never be just my friend.*

'Can I get anything else for you two?' A smiling Darlene set two steaming scones with jam and cream on the table in front of Steve.

'Thanks,' he said. 'We're fine.'

No, Anneliese confirmed, her teeth clenching as she watched the creases in his cheeks deepen. They were not fine— at least she wasn't. Just look at him smiling at Darlene with that irresistible Anderson charm!

No, he couldn't be just her friend. There were too many hormones in the way, too many emotions to guard against. A heart to protect. Because last night when he'd kissed her, something had happened. Something she'd never felt before had woken inside her and she knew she'd never feel the same again.

It had scared her witless.

She'd made up her mind then and there to keep their relationship polite, agreeable and as distant as possible until they reached Surfers. At least there she'd have her own space, her own bed, and she wouldn't be falling asleep on his shoulder.

He'd be gone.

'Getting back to our conversation,' he said, cutting his scone when Darlene had walked away, 'you don't trust me quite yet, then.'

She looked up and met his eyes. 'Just because we shared a kiss…' She trailed off, heat rushing to her cheeks.

His lips quirked. 'Kiss?'

Her fingers tightened on her cup. The one he'd told her to forget. The one that left all others in the shade. 'It's forgotten. Right?'

'I wasn't talking about the kiss.' He slathered jam and cream on his scone. 'If you change your mind about whatever it is that's bothering you, I'm here.'

If they'd been standing, Anneliese was certain she'd have swayed towards him. Lucky for her, a metre-wide table separated them. She gave a small nod and concentrated on finishing her cooling coffee. Telling Steve was not an option.

Hopefully this ordeal would be over in a few hours. She'd check into the apartment she'd already booked, wave him goodbye and he'd be on his way to Brisbane. Then she wouldn't have to see him again, at least until they were both back in Melbourne. Surely she could manage until then?

They'd been driving an hour when a cramp in her leg forced Anneliese to pull over.

'What's wrong?' A drowsy Steve pushed up in the passenger seat, squinting and reaching for his sunglasses.

'Nothing. Needed a stretch.' She opened her door, climbed out and rubbed the backs of her legs. The fresh breeze and sunshine invigorated her. A subtle movement in the grass caught her attention. She couldn't help herself—wary, she stepped closer. 'Oh, no.'

'What?' Steve said, unfolding himself from the passenger side as she turned back to the car.

'There's something near the base of that tree,' she called. 'Something small and furry. I think it's a sick animal.'

He shrugged. 'What do you think you're going to do about it?'

'Something at least.' She hurried back to the car, reached behind her seat. Grabbing her fur-lined jacket, her favourite cashmere jumper and an old towel from the back seat, she approached the animal. 'It's a young koala.'

'Careful.' Steve drew up alongside her, taking charge as he crouched down. 'They're not the cuddly little critters you think they are. All teeth and claws. Let me—'

'I've got it.' She spoke softly as she tossed her jumper at Steve, then wrapped the towel around her hands for protection. 'Throw this over its head.'

'Cashmere? It'll be ruined.'

'Any other brilliant suggestions?'

A noise similar to a screaming baby emanated from beneath the jumper as together they wrapped the wriggling form firmly.

'About seven months old,' she estimated. 'Probably still partially on mother's milk.'

'How do you know?' Steve asked while he tried to figure how a girl like Anneliese and wildlife fitted. They didn't.

'I've worked with Aussie wildlife sanctuaries. Here, hold it a moment.'

She pulled her jacket on, buttoned it up, then took the bundle from Steve's hands and scooped it inside, close to her chest. 'It needs warmth. We have to get it to the nearest vet. You drive.'

'So it's not only the stuffed furry variety you can't abandon,' he said when they were on their way again.

'I often think I have a better rapport with animals than I do with people.' She lifted a hand and covered her nose, at the moment chock-full of the odour of eucalyptus and strong urine. 'When we were in Africa last year I signed up for a volunteer program at the Cheetah Conservation Fund Centre in Namibia. It was rough, dirty and I loved every minute. It was one of my favourite holidays.'

His quick glance might have held the amazement she'd heard in his voice, and perhaps a dawning respect, except she couldn't see behind his sunglasses.

'You imagined my idea of a holiday is lying on Waikiki Beach.' A smile touched her lips. 'I like that, too.'

'Fred the magpie's one of your orphans?'

'Yes. You'll have to come home and meet him some time. He can't fly but he's personality plus.'

'I'd like that.'

And Anneliese realised she'd like that, too. She also realised that for the past little while they'd been sharing something resembling an easy, uncomplicated camaraderie.

Friends.

Only friends, she told herself, surprised at her sudden change-about in the last couple of hours. Anything else was off limits.

With his eyes firmly on the road, he reached out and rubbed the bump in her jacket. Then his fingers brushed hers and the tension that had eased in her body kicked back in.

But he didn't seem to notice. Or perhaps he did, because she thought his hand curled around the steering wheel a little harder. Nice hands, she thought. Wide, thick-wristed. Sexy. And wondered how they'd look against her belly.

She jerked her head away and saw trees whizzing past her unfocused vision. Just when she thought she'd been doing so well with the friends thing.

'You like causes,' Steve said a few minutes later. 'Save the Whales, Hug a Tree.'

She nodded. 'Passion, more like.'

'You never thought of studying vet science?'

She shrugged. 'My parents hoped I could step into Dad's shoes one day.'

'That's why you help out in his surgery and volunteer at the cardiac unit?'

Where she'd met Cindy when her father had had his transplant. 'Yes.'

'It's not what you want.'

'Of course I do.' She struggled to put the appropriate enthusiasm into her voice. Then shook her head when it failed dismally. 'No. I want to be a vet. I was accepted into a course in Sydney five years back, but Mum got sick…'

She didn't tell him how her mum always got sick whenever Anneliese talked about moving interstate. Whenever she took more than a couple of weeks away from home. Since Mum's death the guilt had come down hard on her—perhaps her mother really had been ill on those occasions that had always coincided with when Anneliese had tried to take a break. Be independent.

'There's still time to study,' Steve said, then pulled into a parking spot. 'We're here.' He switched off the engine, tossed his sunglasses on the dash.

She saw his gaze track over the koala bulge to the collar of her blouse beneath her jacket. The top button had come undone in the fracas. He noticed.

'Pity about your blouse…' He caressed the expensive silk sleeve between his fingers. Eyed the buttons and looked as if he was thinking something she knew would be blush-worthy, but all he said was, 'Bet it cost a few quid, too,' then leaned over her and pushed open the car door. 'Vet's open.'

As they cruised out of town Steve rolled down the window and blasted the air-con, but it didn't help. 'I'm sorry to be the one to tell you, but…'

'I know.' She blew out a disgusted breath. 'This blouse has to go.'

His ongoing fantasy was about to be put to rest. He thought about offering to help, but, even in jest, it wasn't an option. Not with Anneliese. 'We passed a public convenience a street or two back if you want to change.'

'Yes, please.'

When she exited the building she was wearing jeans and a fitted lavender T-shirt, sparking a different but no less entertaining fantasy.

She didn't head for the passenger side, but rounded the engine and stood at the driver's door, her hands on her hips. Not that he was looking at her hands. He just assumed they were on her hips because it was her softly rounded breasts, an eye-catching few inches away from his face through the open window, that had his attention.

Even as he watched, her nipples rose in the fresh breeze, poking at the fabric. He practically salivated. And so close he fancied he could almost see the darker colour beneath. *Fancied*, because he didn't linger; he pulled his eyes up. So he told himself he wasn't aware that her breasts rose as she drew in a breath.

When his gaze eventually reached its destination, her eyes met his, presently more green than blue. Just for a moment, heat met heat before she blinked it away and what might have been confusion took its place.

'I don't think I've ever seen you in jeans,' he heard himself say.

She didn't reply, just yanked open the door. 'It's my turn to drive.'

He spread his hands. 'Your car—whatever you want.' He caught a very subtle whiff of animal fur as he unfolded himself and stood. As his body brushed against her arm.

'Don't say it—I know.' She slid behind the wheel. 'The sooner we get there, the sooner I can take a shower.'

'Any recommendations from friends and acquaintances for tonight's accommodation?' he asked as the first glimpses of high rises appeared.

Palazzo Versace, perhaps? He was tempted, for one crazy moment, to give his credit card a workout and book a night there—separate rooms, or a two-bedroom suite perhaps—just for the sheer extravagant hell of it.

She'd be able to soak off the remnants of koala smell in style. The image slow-danced behind his eyes and into his blood-stream. Plenty of room in that big square bathtub for two—a mountain of bubbles, two flutes of champagne, a loaded soap sponge—

'I don't know about you but I've already booked an apart-ment,' she said, wiping away his visions with a bright, self-sat-isfied voice.

'An apartment.'

'I don't know how long I'll be staying. I'd go crazy in a

single motel room. This one's serviced, fully furnished. Own kitchen. *One* bedroom.'

'What's the name?' he asked, already pulling out his mobile.

He dialled call connect for Pacific Paradise Apartments as the road widened, traffic thickened and the buildings grew taller. He intended checking in next door if possible.

Next door to Anneliese. He slid a sideways glance at her. Her sunglasses shielded her eyes but there was nothing to stop him looking at the neat diamond-studded earlobes that he suddenly ached to close his teeth over. Her soft, rose-tinted lips and reliving how they'd felt against his. Her long fingers with their clear polished nails and imagining them on his body...

He blew out a breath, closed his eyes on the temptation beside him as a woman answered his call, and hoped to heaven the building had strong security.

'We made it,' Anneliese said a short time later as they pulled into the apartment's parking area.

Steve turned to see a smile spreading over her face. A gorgeous smile and uninhibited for once. 'With my navigational skills, did you doubt it?'

'That so doesn't count.' She tapped a finger on the steering wheel. 'You used the phone's GPS and *not* that map in front of you. It was my expertise behind the wheel that got us here an hour before your ETA.'

'True,' he admitted, unable to take his eyes from the way her lips curved, enjoying the almost shy pride in her voice. 'All true.' And he wanted her to enjoy that sense of accomplishment. He had a feeling she didn't experience it often.

But her smile faded as she looked up at the five-storey building, the setting sun painting the white walls crimson, and some of that ongoing tension that seemed to be a core part of their relationship crept back.

She rolled her shoulders as if shaking it away. As if telling herself that after last night anything would be a breeze. That they wouldn't be within touching distance. *Kissing distance.* 'Let's move,' she said, her voice sharpening as she shoved open the door and pushed out.

Steve did the same. The weather was cool, the wind humid and salty on his bare arms as he opened the boot. 'I'll unload if you want to check in first.'

When he met her outside the lobby with her trolley cases, she told him there was a problem with his room and he'd have to sort it out and get his own key.

He glanced at the building. The problem was that she'd booked ahead and prevented him from choosing some place more upmarket than this middling accommodation. A suite of rooms where at least they could share a central area and he could keep an eye out for her. That was going to change, and soon. 'Let's get you settled first,' he said.

Anneliese wrinkled her nose as she pushed the door open. The apartment smelled stuffy and not anywhere near her usual standard, but she hadn't been thinking clearly when she'd booked. The living area overlooked the complex's pool and barbecue area surrounded by tropical foliage.

'Is this all you need for tonight?' Steve steered her largest bag inside. She set her smaller rolling suitcase and shoulder bag down and looked up at him, then wished she hadn't because he was too close, smelling too *male*. Reminding her of last night.

And the silence hummed between them, simmering with possibilities. As if she might need something else. Like the taste of his lips, the feel of his hands on her T-shirt. Beneath her T-shirt. 'I'm fine for now. Thank you.'

'You want to go get something to eat in a while after you've had a shower?'

Yes. The prospect of being alone in an unfamiliar room in

an unfamiliar town held little appeal. Instead of revelling in the freedom she'd always craved, she wanted company. Even Steve's company. Especially Steve's company, she realised with a pulse-stopping jolt.

And that was *exactly* why she said, 'No, thanks. I've got a couple of microwave meals in a box somewhere, then I'm going to catch up on sleep.' Her new life started *now*. 'Thanks for…everything.'

His eyes flickered and she got that he was thinking about that kiss. He lifted a hand to her face, and the pads of his fingers stroked over her cheek and she had an insane urge to cover it with one of her own, to tell him she'd changed her mind about dinner, before he backed away.

'See you in the morning, then,' he said in an easy way that turned her inside out. The smile faded as the intensity in his eyes deepened. He flicked the security chain on the door jamb. 'Lock up behind me.'

The moment the door clicked behind him, she sank weakly onto her suitcase. *Lock up behind me.* With that look, had he meant he needed a locked door to keep him away from her? *For heaven's sake, get real.* He was a security freak, that was all.

She slid the chain on. He was probably glad she hadn't accepted his offer of dinner—it gave him the opportunity to explore the night spots. Knowing him, she wouldn't be at all surprised if he got lucky tonight. And she was *not* going to examine how she felt about that.

CHAPTER SIX

HERE we go again.

Rather, there they *go again.* Anneliese rolled her eyes at the ceiling as the rhythmic thud increased. Obviously her neighbours didn't need any sleep because this was the third time tonight she'd been woken to the sounds of sex against the adjoining wall.

As if she knew what sex sounded like. Heat spread through her body and her T-shirt chafed against suddenly sensitised skin as the rhythm gathered pace and feminine moans joined the chorus.

She pulled her pillow around her ears. When she listened again—not that she was trying—she heard muffled laughter. At least someone was happy.

Shoving a hank of hair from her eyes, she glanced at her clock. Seven-thirty. Snuggling down again, she wondered idly what it would be like to wake next to another person. Or—more interesting—to be *woken* by that person… In all manner of ways. And that man would have silky dark hair that flopped onto her forehead when he kissed her good morning. And his eyes would be brown, with just a fleck of honey.

She heard the adjacent apartment's door shut and sat up to watch the girl climb into her car and drive away. Collapsing back onto her pillow, she stared at the ceiling, restless and dissatisfied.

Because the very man she'd been imagining had slipped into her dreams again, all big and bad and beautiful. She slapped her hands on the mattress on either side of her. What else was new? He'd been slipping uninvited into her dreams for the past three years, making her waking life, when he was around, an exercise in humiliation. Rather than the quiet, calm and confident woman she usually was, she tripped over her words—when she could untie her tongue in the first place—blushed, and generally behaved like an adolescent schoolgirl.

So she should be feeling good about herself this morning. She'd managed two days and one long night no more than an arm's length away from him and survived with most of her dignity intact. She'd discovered she could hold a reasonably intelligent conversation with him. She'd barely blushed at all yesterday.

They were friends of sorts. Which came as something of a shock. Had she misjudged him all these years? Was he really the 'nice guy' she'd witnessed over the past couple of days? Hardly, she scoffed to herself, with his female admiration society.

But something more had happened than the beginnings of some kind of friendship. The spark between them had flared into more of a brush fire. She knew it; he knew it. She'd seen it in his eyes more than once over the past couple of days.

Maybe it had always been there—she'd never dared look at him that closely.

Or maybe she was seeing what she wanted to see. She was imagining that kiss to be more than it was... Whatever *that* was...

Letting Steve Anderson into her life would be a fatal mistake. For one, she couldn't imagine his big body perched on those uncomfortably tiny antique chairs in the formal lounge and drinking tea out of Mum's eggshell fragile cups. Or suffering through one of those stuffy hospital charity events she felt obliged to attend that served white wine and cucumber triangle sandwiches.

And none of that would matter because her family life was about to be turned more upside down than it already was. She only hoped that by the time she went home she'd have her life under some kind of control. Steve would make that impossible.

The knock at the door had her scooting off the bed and searching for something to cover herself. She'd been too tired to even look at her suitcase last night and after ringing her father to say they'd arrived safely she'd showered and gone to bed in a T-shirt and panties she'd dug out of her overnighter.

'I'm coming,' she called, and, wrapping herself in her quilt, she padded to the door and pulled it open.

Steve. Looking bed-tumbled and…bad…in black jeans and T-shirt with his hair flopping over an eyebrow and two days' worth of dark stubble. Her heart took a somersault. She forgot her reasons for keeping him at a distance. She wanted to be close. Close enough to stroke his face the way the sunlight did, accentuating strong lines and golden skin.

Then she noticed he had a box from a fast-food outlet in his hand…and a frown on his face.

With the prospect of breakfast tempting her nostrils, she ignored the frown and smiled, her stomach growling its appreciation as the fragrance of coffee and bacon wafted upwards. 'Hi.'

His frown deepened as his gaze swept down. 'Do you always answer the door like that?'

Like that—she saw a flash of heat singe the edges of his cool demeanour and followed his gaze. Her cheeks burned as she made a fumbling attempt to cover a long expanse of bare thigh. And she'd been doing so well with the blushing thing.

His gaze shifted to her face, but clearly his mind was on the peep-show she'd just given him. 'That, too,' he said, and cleared his throat. 'But what I *meant* was opening the door without checking who's there first. Didn't I tell you to lock up behind me?'

Her eyes slid to the security chain. 'I forgot. I had to get my quilt and pillow out of the car—I didn't like the smell of the sheets.' Nor did she like his authoritarian tone. Her enthusiasm at seeing him took a dive. 'I'm fine and it's broad daylight.'

He blew out a breath as if to say, *Have it your way. For now.* She suspected Steve wasn't a man who gave up easily. He'd be the type to turn up again tonight after she'd gone to bed just to check if she'd put the chain on. And maybe next time she wouldn't wrap herself in the quilt either…

'May I come in?'

She blinked in the sunlight and realised she was still blocking the doorway and that she was letting her imagination run away with her again. *Get a grip.* 'You brought breakfast, of course you can.' Holding the edges of her quilt together, she backed away. 'Um…I'll just…find my jeans.'

Steve watched her disappear into the bedroom. His breathing was elevated and sweat tracked down his back as if he'd sprinted ten kilometres rather than the brisk jog to the nearest take-away.

How come he hadn't known about the legs? A long, smooth stretch of temptation, all the way to…paradise.

And she'd opened the door without a care in the world, an invitation to any stranger who might have come knocking. His fingers tightened on the breakfast box. How she conducted her life shouldn't concern him.

And yet one glimpse of her face glowing with health and devoid of make-up wiped his mind. He'd forgo bacon burgers and hash browns for a month for one sweet bite of her naked lips. He shook his head, set the box on the table, then searched cupboards for plates. If he had any sense of self-preservation he'd dump the breakfast and sprint that ten kilometres along the beach—better yet, all the way back to Melbourne.

If Anneliese had any sense of self-preservation that might be possible.

'Mmm. I must be hungry if take-away smells glorious,' Anneliese said, appearing at the doorway, finger-combing her hair behind her ears.

His hand paused in the act of reaching for china. Jeez… She was wearing another one of those thin T-shirts. The kind she'd worn yesterday. The kind you could practically see through.

And nothing else beneath.

His hands tingled, his mouth watered. Blood rushed to his groin. Grabbing two plates, he crossed the room in three strides and sat down fast to hide the rapidly growing evidence. 'I got fruit salad, two burgers, hash browns and two coffees.' He pulled out each item, dumped them on the table, then unwrapped a burger with quick jerky movements.

She raised a brow at his brusque manner, sat opposite him and took the lid off a coffee. 'Not enough sleep?'

'I slept just fine.' Until he'd woken in the early hours with a hard-on to end all hard-ons. And the only thing he was likely to get intimately acquainted with was his cold shower. He'd also wondered how she was doing three floors down, cursing the concierge's ineptitude and hoping he'd sleep better tonight knowing he was in the room next to Anneliese. He sampled his own coffee and made an effort to control the frustration in his voice. 'You?'

'Great.' If he hadn't glanced up he'd have missed the flicker in her sea-green eyes as she asked, 'Are you leaving for Brisbane today?'

He returned his concentration to his breakfast, keeping his

eyes well away from the view across the table. 'No. I've got a few days up my sleeve. Don't worry.' He waved a hand. 'I won't get in the way of whatever it is you're planning.'

He didn't expect a response and none was forthcoming. 'Listen, Anneliese. You might as well know now—I am not leaving Surfers Paradise until I know you're okay. So why don't you just come clean about your plans?'

'Why don't you just leave me alone?' She lifted the lid on the fruit, dug in with the plastic spoon provided and lifted a slice of fresh mango to her mouth.

And for his own self-preservation, he was *not* going to watch. 'No can do.'

Anneliese exhaled a resigned breath. Why was he making this so damn hard? 'I haven't made up my mind what I'm doing yet.'

His expression as he met her eyes turned cold. 'So you're here for the sun and shopping after all.' He shook his head. 'You really are something else.'

No! she wanted to shout. She needed to check out where her sister worked and somehow find the courage to meet her. He must have mistaken her response as one of indifference. She couldn't explain and he'd never understand if she didn't. Perhaps it was better this way—let him think the worst of her and leave her in peace. 'So go, just go,' she said.

Scoffing down the last bite of burger, he crushed the wrapper in his fist and dropped it on the table. He picked up his coffee, his chair scraping as he pushed back and rose.

She noticed he didn't pick up any of the greasy food he'd brought. 'Don't you want any more of this food?'

'Food? That's all you have to say?' He waved her off without so much as a glance. 'Stick it in the fridge. Microwave it for lunch after your swim or whatever whim you choose to indulge in.' His sneakers squeaked over the tiles as he crossed to the door and his voice was as biting as an Antarctic wind. 'Have a nice day.'

Anneliese sat back in her chair, staring at the door long after he'd gone, half expecting to see him pop back in. Five minutes later, she tipped the remains of her coffee down the sink and frowned out at the tropical morning. She'd got what she wanted, hadn't she? Steve out of her life.

But it didn't make her happy or relieved.

Late that afternoon Anneliese dumped the groceries she'd bought and a couple of sightseeing brochures on the table and made herself a pot of chamomile tea. Why she'd bought a packet of chamomile tea when she'd never tried it, she had no idea, but she waited for it to brew while she checked out the local restaurant guide for dinner.

She'd spent the day walking. Thinking. Soul-searching. And everywhere she went she wondered if the woman standing beside her was her sister. She found herself looking at faces for something familiar—in the eyes, the hair, the bone structure.

Did Abigail remember their mother? Did she, too, hurt at being abandoned? Anneliese sat at the table and poured her tea wondering what kind of upbringing her sister had had. How she'd ended up in Surfers Paradise working in a boutique hotel.

Of course, her thoughts led straight to the only parents she'd known, and that had her up and pacing, mug in hand. Yes, she mourned her mum. And Dad—she was racked with guilt about what she was doing. She'd tried to ease it by phoning him regularly, but hearing his voice... She wandered to the window to watch the sky turn from pink to lavender and see the early evening lights come on.

And her breath caught. Steve hadn't left Surfers, as she'd expected, and she was torn between conflicting feelings of doom and delight. There he was, accessorising her car to per-

fection, black vest over his T-shirt, his long denim-clad legs
crossed at the ankles while he watched her apartment and
talked on his mobile. Her heart performed its familiar aerobics
as she studied him through the sheer curtain.

What better guy to imprint his very fine backside on her car
door than Steve Anderson? Now if she was to head outside and
meet him... Manoeuvre it so that she was against the car...
She'd be pressed between the cool smooth metal and the hard-
muscled heat of his body... A tingle danced down her back.

She tore her gaze away. Stupid to let those crazy thoughts get
the better of her. Stupid and a waste of energy. After this morning,
his respect for her must be zilch. But she hadn't been mistaken
about the heat she'd seen in his eyes before they'd had words.

He slid the phone into his pocket and headed for the
building, but he didn't knock as she expected. He passed right
by, then she heard the sound of a key turning in the adjacent
apartment, the door closing behind him.

The apartment whose bedroom adjoined hers.

The bedroom where all the action had taken place.

And the guy she'd been fantasising about, even as he'd kept
her awake half the night with his sexual games, was *Steve*.

It took a few shocked seconds for the knowledge to unlock
her brain and connect to the rest of her body. A different kind
of heat swept through her. A horrible, nauseating kind that
rolled around like ball lightning, battering her till she thought
she might have to throw up.

Leaning against the wall, she scrubbed her hands over her
sweaty brow. Of course he had women. Why had she expected
him to curtail his sexual activities on her account? Why was it
different now?

Because now she knew how he kissed, how he tasted. How
his hands felt on her skin, the heat and strength and shape of
his body against hers.

The ringing tones of her mobile on the table jerked her out of her thrall and she realised she was standing in semi-darkness. She let it ring until it diverted to message bank before she listened. It was Steve, checking if she was back yet.

He'd probably knock on her door at any moment. She couldn't let him see her like this, nor did she want to see him. Pushing away from the wall, she concentrated on putting one foot in front of the other until she reached her bedroom.

She had to get out before he knew she was back. Anywhere. She flung open the wardrobe, grabbed a black and blue patterned silk dress, shimmying into it as she stepped into open black and gold stilettos, then picked up her bag.

Again she left her car in favour of walking and ten minutes later she was lost amongst the crowd on Cavill Avenue. This was where she wanted to be—on the street with the highest concentration of licensed venues in Australia, far away from her problems and the man she didn't want to think about. Lights glittered, neon signs flashed, but it was too early for the night crowd. She chose a bar at random. At this time of the evening it wasn't crowded and she hitched herself onto a stool and ordered a glass of chardonnay.

An hour later, still on her first glass, she'd compared travel notes with Simone from Sydney and chatted to a waitress who doubled as an exotic dancer at midnight.

Then a nice guy by the name of Randy, a perfect gentleman really—a casting agent from San Francisco, he'd told her—had bought her the prettiest cocktail: blue and green with a lemon wedge on the side.

But now she wasn't feeling so good and her head felt fuzzy and when she heard her phone ring she answered it immediately.

'Where the hell are you?' The bark on the other end sounded rough-edged and familiar.

'Steve.' She twirled the little stick in her almost-full drink, watching blue swirl into green and remembering last night's audio show. And he thought he had the right to make demands on her?

'Haven't you listened to your voice messages? I've called six times. We had a dinner reservation.' His words were clipped and curt.

'I'm in a bar—I didn't hear the phone. I wasn't aware we were—'

'In a bar? Are you alone?'

'Are you?' Her attempt at a sassy reply came out slurred and she gripped the bar for support as dizziness swamped her.

'Tell me where you are.' He spoke each word slowly and they seemed to echo from a distance.

'On Cavill Avenue.' She looked about for Randy but he'd moved to a table of guys. He gave her a nod, a grin, and turned to his mates and suddenly he didn't look so nice.

'What's the name?' said the voice in her ear.

'I didn't see…' She squinted at the entrance which seemed an impossible distance away. 'It has one of those neon signs, a green cocktail glass out fr—'

'Stay right there. Don't move.'

He disconnected and Anneliese let out a slow steadying breath. Except she wasn't steady. Nothing was steady, nothing at all.

Steve shoved his mobile in his pocket and sprinted towards Cavill Avenue, weaving his way through a mix of casually attired tourists and those out for an evening of clubbing.

Angry tension tightened with disappointment every passing second. Still the same typical Anneliese. Irresponsible and self-centred, doing what she damn well pleased without a thought for anyone else. She hadn't even bothered responding to his messages.

Keeping his eyes peeled for the green cocktail glass, he barely noticed the kaleidoscope of flash and colour and aromas. He should've gone straight to Brisbane. He'd be wining and dining his way through his list of new clients by now, not baby-sitting some girl who wouldn't grow up.

The fact that alarm was coiling its way around his anger only ticked him further.

The green sign caught his eye and his sigh of relief and annoyance hissed out between clenched teeth. She wore a demure black and blue silk dress with puffed sleeves, but its short skirt rode high on her hips, showcasing those gorgeous legs. Sophisticated innocence? But this pale-faced Anneliese wasn't the bright-eyed girl he'd left this morning. A cab back, then.

He fought the ridiculous impulse to wrap her up in his arms and protect her. That urge had only ever given him grief in the past. Instead he tapped her shoulder.

She turned, glazed eyes meeting his, and something like a fish-hook snared him mid-chest. He had the sinking feeling he'd forgive her anything if she asked.

What looked like relief twitched at the corner of her mouth. 'Steve.'

'Princess,' he mocked as he lifted a hand in the direction of the door. 'Your chariot awaits.'

He didn't know where the title sprang from or if it hit home, but it damn well wasn't lost on him. Her shoulders slumped as she leaned into him, her head dropping onto his shoulder. Then she sighed, a soft sound that seemed to come from the depths of her being, and slid her arms around his neck. 'I'm so glad you're here,' she whispered, then slid off the stool and down every hard, hot, aching inch of his body. 'Please take me home.'

Nor do I need someone holding my hand and tucking me into bed at night.

She did tonight, he thought grimly, scooping her into his arms. The million-dollar question was whose bed was he going to tuck her into?

CHAPTER SEVEN

HAILING a cab, Steve deposited Anneliese on the seat and slid in beside her. For now he ignored the smell of booze overlaying her perfume as her head slid against his shoulder. She was in no condition to pack up and move to the new hotel he'd booked them into, but at least he had her back safely.

As he'd assured Marcus in his phone call to her father earlier in the day.

He'd rung only to check on the man's well-being since his irresponsible daughter might well have forgotten. Apparently she'd rung twice a day every day. 'I know now why she's there, Steve,' he'd told him. 'She doesn't know I've discovered her reasons and I'd prefer to keep it that way, but, believe me, she has every right. I'm the one at fault here, but it's her story, her place to tell you, not mine. You don't know how much I appreciate you being nearby. It takes a load off my mind.'

So now, it seemed, Steve had inherited some sort of responsibility. He couldn't ignore his relief that Anneliese wasn't the heartless, selfish girl he'd been beginning to think she was. There was a reason for her behaviour, even if she wasn't inclined to tell him. A reason her father considered a valid one. He had to accept Marcus's word, though he doubted it included public drunkenness.

A few moments later he was propping her up outside her door. Her knees seemed to sag until she was draped over him like a rag doll and he wanted nothing more than to burrow into her soft feminine warmth. He clenched his jaw, kept his hands impersonal but supportive. 'Where's your key-card?'

In her bag, of course. He managed to unzip the thing single-handedly and locate the familiar credit-card shape by touch. It was a scenario he was familiar with—women who used intoxication as an excuse to entice him into their bed. He didn't usually have to carry them over the threshold, but in this case it seemed the most expedient method. As he scooped her up she seemed to snuggle against him and he tried not to imagine the same scene under different circumstances. Taking a willing Anneliese to his own bed, seeing the anticipation build in her eyes as he laid her down. Watching passion flare in those eyes as he stretched out beside her, skimmed his hand over her body...

Thank heavens her eyes were closed. 'Okay, bedtime.' He kept his voice brisk as he pulled back her quilt and sat her on the mattress. She promptly slumped back onto the pillow. With the curtains not yet drawn the lights outside lanced through the window—plenty of light to see the dark circles beneath her eyes as she looked up at him. He tried not to think about the slender shape of her ankles as he slipped her shoes off.

'I feel...like... Bad.'

He set his hands on his hips and nodded. 'That'll teach you to drink to excess.'

'One glass...'

Laughable. 'I don't think so. You lost count.'

'No.' Her blurry eyes widened. 'And a cocktail Randy bought me...'

Steve pulled up sharp. 'Randy? Who's Randy?'

'He...don't r'member.'

Instantly he sat down beside her, turned on the lamp beside the bed and brushed a tendril of damp hair from her brow, his hand tightening as he took in the sight and the implications: drink-spiking, date rape. 'How much did you have of this *cocktail*?'

'Only a sip. Looked pretty, but...didn't like it.'

'I'm going to make you coffee,' he told her. 'I won't be long. Then I'm going to stay here with you until you feel better. Okay?'

She made a murmur of consent and closed her eyes.

Steve boiled the kettle and ripped open the coffee sachet, but his mind was back in the bar, searching remembered glimpses of faces as he'd scanned the room for Anneliese.

His jaw clenched as he poured water over coffee, added cold to lower the temperature. *I'll kill him.* Except he hadn't a hope in hell of finding him. The low-life who'd taken advantage of a naïve young woman on her own.

He found her as he'd left her, eyes closed. He needed her awake long enough to get her to drink. 'Here.' He slid an arm around her shoulders and drew her up against his body, then placed the cup between her hands, covered them with his. 'Slow, now.'

She took a sip. 'You don't have to...' Her eyes pooled with moisture. 'Stay, I mean. If you have...something else, some-one...to...'

'What are you talking about? If you'd bothered listening to my messages—all six of them—we had a dinner date.'

'A date? You and me?'

'Dinner,' he corrected. It was all in the emphasis. 'Drink up and I'll let you sleep.'

'Lights.' She gazed up at him as she sipped. 'Around your head. Like a halo.'

He glanced at the coloured lights from the convenience

store across the road. 'Guardian angels always have a halo.' His smile was forced; he'd never felt less honest in his life.

Right this minute he wanted her in every *un*angelic way he knew. He took the still half-full mug from her hands and set it on the night-stand. 'You'll feel more comfortable if we take off your dress.'

Her eyes widened and he shook his head. 'Why don't you let me undo the zip, then I'll turn my back and let you do the rest?'

She nodded, her teeth biting into her lower lip. Her eyes locked with his as he lifted her hair, and darkened to emerald when he leaned closer.

Torture not to lean the rest of the way and soothe her lips with his. Torture as the back of his hand connected with the warmth of her neck, the sound of the zip as he tugged it down, his knuckles grazing vertebrae, a ridge of bra clasp, and finally the smooth curve of her lower back.

And, heaven help him, he wanted to lay his burning mouth on the pale skin he revealed between neck and shoulder as he drew the edges of her dress away. To slide his fingers beneath the black bra straps, ease them down to her waist and taste the sweetness of those full breasts.

Pulling back, he stared at her for a long moment, drinking in her fragile beauty.

Her *vulnerability*.

That recognition slid under his skin like flint and changed everything. She needed a friend, not a lover. But the mere thought of the latter sent his pulse galloping. Raw with a rising frustration, he muttered, 'You can manage the rest, I think.'

Despite the jaw-tensing control, heat continued to pool in his groin as he heard the soft shoosh of flesh against fabric. He concentrated on watching the lights across the road flash blue to red to blue again until the movement behind him ceased.

When he turned, she lay on her side, hugging the quilt to her chin, and was looking at him through dark glazed eyes. 'Thanks,' she murmured. 'All right now.' Even as he watched, the eyelids drooped, her mouth softened, her breathing slowed.

He continued to watch her. She was *not* all right. God only knew what she'd ingested. He'd promised Cindy, and her father, and himself, to be here for her. He toed off his shoes, shucked his vest, then walked around the bed to the other side to switch off the lamp.

Easing himself gingerly onto the empty space beside her, he stretched out on his back, his arms behind his head, trying not to breathe in the scent of her pillow, *not* imagining stripping off his clothing and sliding beneath the quilt with her. *Bodyguard, remember.*

Instead he gritted his teeth and directed his mind elsewhere. Somewhere cold and desolate and far, far away.

As Anneliese surfaced from sleep she knew something was different before she opened her eyes. The deep, even sound of someone breathing in her ear... Her eyes snapped open as she swivelled her head on the pillow.

The dull throb in her temples barely registered. Steve lay alongside her, one hand beneath his cheek, his breathing warm against her face. Her own breath caught, stalled, then came out in a rush. She didn't know if it was possible to be panicked and relieved at the same time.

She'd never woken up with a man before—she'd never slept with a man either—but Steve Anderson, dream inspirer, fantasy weaver, was sleeping next to her. Inches from her. In her bed. Sharing the same air.

And looking every bit the fantasy that kept her awake nights. Dark stubble shadowed his jaw, giving him that rakish appearance, over-long hair curled around his ear. Early morning's pink light painted his skin and etched angular lines into his strong facial planes.

So it took a few more heart-stopping seconds for the fact that she was beneath the quilt, and he was not, to register. Another few to notice he was fully clothed.

And she was not.

Oh. My. God. What have I done? What have *we* done?

Then the evening rushed back in a sickening blur. But Steve hadn't done anything even remotely untoward when he'd carried her to her bed. He'd been the perfect gentleman. She'd always thought the words 'gentleman' and 'Steve' mutually exclusive.

Then the reason why she'd rushed off flashed through her mind. Not that she'd asked to be rescued, she thought darkly. Or maybe she had… She couldn't quite remember. Still…he might be a perfect gentleman with her, but with other women… He was that dream lover with other women. Just not with Anneliese Duffield.

And that fanned yesterday afternoon's anger and burning frustration all over again. She huffed a sigh, surprised she wasn't breathing fire. Told herself she did *not* want him to be dangerous with her. She had more important things on her mind, like meeting her sister.

She must have disturbed him because he stirred and shifted. One hard thigh moved, pinning her to the mattress. Then a bare sinewy arm slid over her abdomen, curved around her waist and pulled her closer.

Her heart rate sped up. Her own bare skin prickled beneath her quilt and she squirmed against the sudden spurt of heat low in her belly.

Then his lashes fluttered, he blinked, and a pair of brown velvet eyes stared into hers. A momentary confusion vanished, replaced by concern as he lifted the hand around her waist to brush the hair from her brow and touch her cheek.

Given their current circumstances, it was such an intimate gesture. Kind of like what she'd imagined him to do after... She shook away the image. 'I'm fine,' she assured him. 'No side effects.' Unless she counted the one his presence in her bed was having on her.

His expression cleared, and a corner of his mouth lifted. 'In that case, good morning, princess.' His morning voice rumbled in the mattress and vibrated through her body.

'Good morning.'

He made no move to get up, or to remove his thigh from on top of hers. He seemed content to lie and watch her as the room brightened and tropical birds sang outside the window.

Or maybe 'content' and 'watch' weren't the right words after all because a few seconds later he propped his head up on one elbow, those velvet eyes unreadable, and said, 'So perhaps you're feeling up to explaining why you stood me up last night without a word.'

Her stomach bottomed out; her throat dried up. 'I thought you'd prefer her company, given the good time you two had the previous night. Or if you—'

'What the *hell* are you talking about?'

She withdrew a hand from beneath the quilt and tapped on the wall behind her head.

He looked at her blankly. 'You've lost me.'

'The bed next door abuts mine. Think about it, Steve. The *bed*. Bed springs. Two people. I'm sure you get the picture.'

She watched comprehension dawn in his dark eyes. She didn't know what she expected him to say, but she didn't expect him to laugh.

But he did. He threw back his head, his rich chuckles echoing off the ceiling.

She'd never felt so humiliated. So ridiculously hurt. She wanted to pull the quilt over her head and never have to face him again. Pressing her lips together, she turned to the window.

The laughter faded. 'It wasn't me.'

'Oh, come on.' Her voice trembled out. 'I saw you let yourself in there yesterday afternoon.'

'The desk staff couldn't fit me in that room when we arrived. That was the key problem they told you about. I had a room three storeys up. I only moved next door lunch-time yesterday.'

'Oh.' *Great. Just great. What a fool.* Somehow right now even that news didn't make her feel better; she still wanted to pull the quilt over her head—with embarrassment. She'd exposed a part of herself she tried never to allow anyone to see. Vulnerability. Stupidity.

A thumb and forefinger pinched her chin and turned her to him. He was sitting up now and his eyes still twinkled with amusement. She tried to drag his fingers away, but his free hand grabbed hers and held tight.

'Oh, Annie…' Then he slid his thumb over her bottom lip, a sensuous caress that filled her with fear, with longing, and her hand fell away of its own accord.

Then he twisted, placing his arms on the bed to either side of her, trapping her beneath her quilt. The mirth in his eyes faded, as if he'd seen that raw, vulnerable space around her heart, and something deeper took its place. A look that said, *I want to kiss you. And this time I don't want you to push me away.*

She'd fantasised about Steve looking at her the way he was looking at her now. Not as his sister's friend, not as a spoilt rich chick.

But as a desirable woman.

She saw something that soothed the jagged peaks of dazzle and danger of letting a man like Steve into her life. Something she could take purchase on.

He leaned over…and his lips were warm and dry, firm yet gentle. Anneliese gave in to the moment and closed her eyes on that slow, sensual kiss that lingered for what seemed like eternity.

Gave in to more as he murmured something soft and low against her mouth. She didn't hear the words but their message hummed through her senses as his tongue traced her lips, then gently urged them apart, filling her mouth with his taste. Inviting her to join him in this dreamy delicious pleasure she'd never experienced with any other man.

His lips left hers and she almost moaned the loss, but he wasn't through; he tracked a path over her cheek, her chin, an ear. The sensitive hollow beneath her jaw. Sweet, open-mouthed kisses that left her skin tingling with pleasure.

And then he was moving over her shoulders, soothing the damp daisy patches of skin he left behind with his fingers, until his tongue found the top of her bra. Until he smoothed the quilt down her torso and cupped her breasts in his hands, closed his mouth around an areola through the soft black lace.

Her nipple hardened and puckered beneath the gentle tug of his teeth. Heat slammed through her. Her breath backed up in her lungs and she found herself tensing, taut.

Terrified.

Terrified because it was as if he'd stolen her will. And that was the danger she'd always known he posed to her. For a brief giddy moment, she'd wanted. Wanted so much it ached. She'd thought she was ready for this. For Steve. For it all.

'Stop,' she whispered, her fingers gripping the quilt at her waist lest he lower it farther and then she'd truly be lost.

He lifted his mouth and looked into her eyes and she wanted to moan that loss and for once in her life to live dangerously, on her own terms. But would it really be her terms, or his? Here, in a paradise of sand and sun, glitz and glamour and tropical nights, romance could sweep you away on its tide and leave you stranded.

'I didn't come here for this,' she said, struggling to pull up the quilt.

'It's okay, Anneliese.' He tugged the quilt up gently. 'I must've misread the signals. I thought that's what you wanted.'

It is, she wanted to shout. *I've wanted it for so long I don't even know if this moment is reality or a dream any more.*

He smoothed the fabric beneath her chin. A spark of his desire lingered in his eyes, banked but still smouldering.

'We're just friends, remember?' she all but whispered.

'Friends.' He made an impatient noise in his throat.

'If you don't mind, I want to take a shower…' She blinked away a vision of the two of them naked and wet. Together.

He stared at her a moment longer, then nodded, bent to retrieve his shoes and put them on. 'We're checking out this morning. I've booked us somewhere more comfortable.'

Us? As in they were going to be sharing a room? As in he'd taken it upon himself to make decisions without telling her? 'You *what*?' Dragging the quilt with her, she jackknifed up.

'Calm down, princess.' He sauntered to the chair, picked up his vest. 'It's a two-bedroom suite.'

'You go ahead. I've arranged my own change of accommodation. And don't call me princess.'

He shrugged on his vest and turned. 'Why not? You're acting like one, and a spoilt one at that. Where are you going to be staying? I'll arrange the change.' Then he walked to the bed and sat down. 'I'll find out whether you tell me or not.'

She had no doubt about that and somehow it no longer mattered. It was simply easier to go with the flow. His body had shifted closer and she found herself falling straight into those bottomless dark eyes. His gaze was the only part of him that touched her, but he seemed to surround her. 'A boutique hotel called Capricorn Centre.'

He nodded. 'I'll make a couple of calls.'

CHAPTER EIGHT

BY MID-MORNING Steve leaned against the balcony of Capricorn Centre's new two-bedroom executive suite and spa, his hand wrapped around a can of soda. Not a large building by any means, but luxury was the key word. Every whim was catered to, which would suit Anneliese down to the ground. She could shop, swim and eat, be pampered, plucked or massaged without leaving the centre. With guest in-house services available she could do most of those things without even leaving their suite if she wanted.

She was indulging already. In the spa built for two. Alone.

Steve tilted his head to the sky, letting the sun's warmth bathe his closed eyelids. Listening to the surf and the sigh of the salt breeze in the casuarinas lining the edge of the property. *Not* thinking about Anneliese in that big spa all by herself.

It didn't escape his attention that if she'd been any other woman sharing his hotel suite, he'd be indulging right along with her.

Sandy—or was it Suzy?—and he had spent the Easter holidays in the penthouse suite in one of Sydney's most exclusive waterfront resorts. The view from the spa had been amazing. The view *in* the spa had been pretty amazing. Four days of good food, good wine and no-strings sex.

He hadn't seen Suzy/Sandy since.

The best way to be. The only way. No one got hurt.

Which in a roundabout way brought him back to Anneliese.

He tried telling himself he'd had itches like this before and no doubt he would again. Except Anneliese Duffield had been the one itch he'd never been able to scratch, and since this morning's kiss that had left him gasping for more, and lying next to her last night with only a quilt separating him from all that bare silky skin and not being able to touch her... Hell.

His eyes were open now and focused on the sea, but he barely saw the sun's sparkle on the blue water. What now? Well, just maybe, he'd get to scratch that itch.

Was that what he wanted? Oh, yeah. His body tensed, his pulse spiked and his fingers tickled against the chilled metal can just thinking about it. But after all that itching and scratching...what then?

Consequences.

The fact that he'd inevitably see her as long as he and Cindy were under the same roof. And the even more disquieting conclusion—one he definitely didn't want to think about—that with Anneliese maybe itching and scratching wouldn't be enough.

No. He shook his head, slammed his free hand on the balcony railing because that one simple—correction: *not-so-simple*—thought twisted his stomach into hard knots of tension. Scraped at scars he'd believed healed. He would not allow himself to go down that road again.

Anneliese stirred feelings he hadn't felt in eight years. Didn't want to feel, ever again.

Because his mouth was suddenly dry, he took a long slug of soda. Caitlyn. A petite, slightly chubby blonde with dancing blue eyes who just made you want to protect her from all the hurts in the world. The kind of woman you could wrap your arms around and hold on to. Someone who'd made him believe a home and family might be possible, even though his mother had dashed that notion when she'd walked out on her husband and kids for some rich guy she'd met on the Internet.

Caitlyn wasn't like his mother. They didn't have much money but they had each other. Right? He let out a humourless snort. He'd never been more wrong.

The can imploded beneath his fingers, sloshing what was left of the liquid over his hand. And *that* fuelled his anger: the fact that Caitlyn and what she'd done still had the power to get to him. Licking the spilt soda from his knuckles, he flopped into a chair nearby. Sometimes life just sucked.

But it wasn't all bad. He still had Cindy. Dad had been gone a couple of years now, which left only his sister. Sometimes he wondered if he shielded her a little too close, but old habits died hard. He'd looked out for Cindy most of his life, which was why he'd kept the old family home—to give her stability and a sense of family in a crazy world that didn't seem to give a damn about those values any more.

He took a deep breath, blew it out slowly, letting go of the old tensions and reminding himself that a wife and home and family were too damn hard and not worth the heartache that came with them. So they were *not* in his life plan.

His intentions hit a snag as Anneliese stepped onto the balcony, a cool temptation in a sunny yellow dress and bare feet. Her auburn hair glinted gold in the sun; damp strands clung to her temples.

She was nothing like Caitlyn. She was tall and dark and willowy. Her eyes didn't dance, they were haunting, and haunted. The aching well inside him grew and squeezed till there was no room left for anything but something that felt like panic.

'I didn't realise you were out here,' she said, looking unsure.

He made a deliberate effort to erase the frown he was suddenly aware of. 'Join me.'

'I think I will. I could do with some sun,' she said, spreading that gorgeous body on the recliner lounge.

Look away, for pity's sake. But his eyes remained riveted on the sight. 'Enjoy yourself?'

He heard a hint of the old mockery in his tone, spliced with a heavy dose of self-disgust because she didn't deserve to be the recipient of his mood.

She either chose to ignore it or didn't notice, because she smiled at him and suddenly the sun seemed to shine a little brighter and, despite the gnawing in his gut, he wanted to smile right back.

So he did, and it felt good. He wanted to be with her. Not only because she was the sexiest woman he'd ever seen, but because for some reason she made him feel happy. She brought something to his life he'd never experienced before. Besides, it wasn't as if it was for ever.

'Oh, yeah, I did,' she sighed, with a slow, sinuous stretch of her limbs. 'I feel almost human again.'

Rather than watch, he moved to the little outdoor table, clicked on his laptop and looked up his contacts in Brisbane. Then he picked up his mobile. With a few calls he spoke to a couple of his major clients, shifted appointments, organised a helicopter charter and a limousine service.

A short time later he leaned back, satisfied that he could juggle work commitments and Anneliese from Surfers, starting with a casual getting-acquainted meeting early this afternoon. The sooner the better, for both of them. Sitting around watching Anneliese wasn't a good idea and he'd promised her he'd stay out of her way to give her time for whatever it was she wanted to do. Steve still wasn't one hundred per cent sure her father wasn't making excuses for her, but what could he do? He had to trust Marcus's judgement and Anneliese.

He shut down his laptop, played restless fingers over the case. 'I'm heading to Brisbane in an hour or so.'

'I didn't think you were starting so soon.' She sounded disappointed, but he couldn't read her eyes because she'd shielded them with her large dark sunglasses.

'It's more of a meet and greet today. The real work begins tomorrow. I'll be gone a couple of hours.' He stretched back in his chair. 'What do you have planned?'

She lifted a shoulder. 'I might go downstairs later. Explore the centre. Maybe indulge in a few guest services. A massage, perhaps.'

Which drew his attention to her exposed skin, as pale and delicate as a Peace rose. He frowned. 'You might want to indulge in some sunscreen if you're going to sit there for much longer.'

For the umpteenth time, her vague plans bothered Steve. She must have heard the doubts in his tone, because she sat up, slid her sunglasses off and fixed him with a wide-eyed stare. 'This hotel wasn't a random choice. I have plans, I just need time.'

'Okay.' He collected his belongings and stood. He had to trust her to tell him the truth, he just wasn't sure if she was stringing him along. 'I'd better make a start, then.'

An invigorating shower later, Steve shrugged into lightweight trousers and a white shirt, freshly pressed thanks to the hotel's efficient laundry service. He'd have to ask Cindy to send extra clothing if he was going to be here for any length of time. And that was the big question—how long did Anneliese intend to stay? Because leaving her in Surfers wasn't an option, and there was the return journey to consider. Perhaps he'd purchase what he needed here, something more suited to the climate. He'd seen a menswear store a few minutes' walk away.

'I'm off, then,' he said, walking out to the patio. Anneliese was asleep with a women's magazine over her face. She'd changed in his absence and was wearing a brief blue and green patterned bikini.

He was male; she was female, and more than half naked. What would any man worth his libido do? It wasn't as if she didn't know he could appear at any time.

But he stopped dead. It wasn't the sight of her glorious long legs that had him rooted to the spot, though that was pulse-stopping enough on its own. Nor was it the slender waist and generous cleavage. Not the compact little navel he'd always wondered about. Fantasised about.

It was the tattoo.

Or what he could see of it. So Anneliese, the very proper Anneliese Duffield, had more than one secret.

Only partially visible where her stomach hollowed out creating a space beneath her bikini bottom, a hand-span's width from her right hip.

He knew it was a hand-span because he could imagine his hand sliding into that space between fabric and sun-warmed skin and easing her bikini down and discovering for himself what she'd chosen to mark her body with.

All this registered in his scrambled brain in under three seconds before he dragged his gaze away.

He curled his fingers into his palms and stared at the cool blue Pacific Ocean while every cell in his body begged for another look. From what he'd seen it looked like some sort of Chinese symbol, but he couldn't be sure. *You don't want to know.*

He continued watching the ocean for a moment until his body's response settled somewhat. With a loud throat-clearing, he stood where he was, then said, 'Anneliese, the limo's here to pick me up. I'll see you later.'

'Huh?' A lazy movement, then she peeled the magazine from her face. 'I fell asleep.' She blinked at him, a quick surprised flick down his body, then her brows puckered as she studied his face. 'Is everything all right?'

He kept his eyes on hers. 'Couldn't be better.' But by crikey it was going to be hard keeping his thoughts from wandering every time she slipped into a bikini. It was going to be hard keeping them from wandering, period. Thank heavens he had something to keep his mind occupied this afternoon.

She stretched her arms up and out as she would when waking up. 'See you later, then.'

Anneliese rolled over onto her stomach and let out a slow breath. Seeing Steve in that snowy white shirt, unbuttoned at the neck, those well-fitted fawn trousers and looking a million dollars... Oh, cripes—it had taken all her restraint to keep her eyes above the neck. Was that the reason her skin tingled with sensation? Or was it because he'd seen her asleep?

She breathed another sigh—of relief this time—that he wasn't hanging around. She didn't need the distraction.

She stayed longer than she intended, soaking up the sun and putting off what she'd told herself she had to do today. Before Steve came back she was going to explore the hotel's shops and services while making some subtle enquiries about Abigail Seymour.

Her skin was beginning to prickle, when she forced herself off the padded recliner and headed inside for a shower. She sprayed her naked body with perfume before slipping back into the yellow sundress. Next she put on white heeled sandals, and took an overly long time styling her hair in the luxury bathroom, then in a last-minute decision she slapped a white sunhat on her head and hid her eyes behind the largest sunglasses she'd been able to find in the local mall yesterday.

She probably looked like a celebrity trying for anonymity, but she felt safer behind the disguise. Her pulse-rate rose as she stepped into the suite's ocean-themed private elevator, which would take her to the ground floor, and let its watery music soothe her jagged nerves.

In the lobby she flicked through a pamphlet featuring the hotel's amenities while gathering her courage to approach a staff member. The larger suites were named after the zodiacal signs and themed accordingly. The Pisces Suite, where she and Steve were staying, was the most recent and most luxurious.

Finally she could put it off no longer. Her heart thumped like fury, her dry mouth turned drier. Her hands shook so she gripped her bag strap with two tight fists. She'd never felt so unprepared for anything in her life. *Calm down*, Anneliese ordered herself. Abigail might not even be working today. And if she was, Anneliese didn't have to expose her own identity. She could assess the situation first, even walk away if she wanted.

With those thoughts, she stepped up to a guy behind the desk whose name tag said he was Dylan.

He placed his hands on the desk and smiled. 'Good afternoon, may I help you?'

'I was wondering if you know where I might find Abigail Seymour. I think she works here, but I don't know if she's in the office or even if she's still here…'

His smile widened and he nodded. 'Abby and Zak Forrester own the hotel. I'm afraid she and Zak are on their honeymoon for a few days.'

'Ah-h-h.' Her whole body breathed a sigh of relief. Abby—she called herself Abby. And she *owned* this place.

'Did you want to leave a message?'

At the sound of his voice, Dylan's face swam back into focus. 'No. Thanks. I'll catch up with her when she gets back.'

Turning, Anneliese headed for the lobby doors and out into the sunshine. All that nervous tension seemed to have drained into her legs. She made it as far as the Norfolk Island Pines where the sea grass lay in untidy flat ribbons on the sand before she let herself collapse in the dappled shade and gulp in the salt-tinged air.

It was only a temporary reprieve. In the next few days she had to psych herself up and do it all over again. She had more time to wait and think and wait some more. What was she going to tell Steve? He was going to think the worst of her. Which probably wasn't a whole lot worse than what he already thought.

Meanwhile they had to share a suite. He might think the worst of her, but their mutual attraction was out on the table for all to see; he'd acknowledged it even if she hadn't. But he knew how she felt. Hadn't he told her that her face was an open book?

Her mobile chimed. She checked the incoming caller as she answered. Speaking of the devil… 'Hi.'

'Annie.' His voice was a seductive dark velvet—the devil with a voice to match. 'There's a cocktail party on tonight. My major client wants to take us out. Other clients will be there, too. Can you be ready in an hour?'

'They want to take *us* out?'

'It's a social occasion. The guys are bringing their wives and partners.'

'But I'm not your…we're not…' She trailed off, confused.

'I told them I came to Queensland with someone and they're expecting you. You're not miles away from the hotel, are you?'

'No, but you're in Brisbane, I'm here.'

'Not a problem. I'll be on my way back in five minutes to change. We'll fly back here when you're ready. Dress code's casually elegant.'

'An *hour*? Are you kidding?' Sixty short minutes to find a suitable dress, iron it, restyle her hair, put on her make-up?

'We can be a little late.' She heard a smile in his voice. 'Say yes, Annie.'

Something to take her mind off her personal problems? He'd been nothing but nice to her; he wouldn't have asked her if he didn't want her along. And she wanted to be with him. *Before you change your mind,* a voice whispered. *Before he changes his mind.* 'Yes.'

'Good. I'll see you soon.'

She disconnected, the hand holding the phone sliding down to her lap, suddenly unsure. *Did* he want to spend the evening with her? Or was it his clients' idea and he felt obligated?

Either way, she wasn't going to disappoint him. She scrambled up, dusted the sand off her feet and headed back to the hotel. She'd seen a gorgeous dress in one of the hotel's boutique shops, and if they had her size...

CHAPTER NINE

ANNELIESE was familiar with this kind of function; she helped organise charity events for the hospital and had no difficulty talking to people she didn't know. The only person she'd ever had difficulty conversing with was Steve, but that was becoming easier with every day they spent together.

Wearing her new designer cocktail outfit, a shell-pink silk calf-length dress with scattered lurex spots that glistened under the night lights when she moved, she felt better than she had in weeks. Its liquid gold lining felt smooth against her skin. The only problem was the spaghetti-thin straps chafing her sunburnt back and shoulders.

Sipping on her peach champagne cocktail, she glanced at Steve, currently engrossed in deep discussion with one of his clients near the floor-to-ceiling windows that looked out onto Brisbane's Botanical Gardens. In his dove-grey suit and silver tie he was the successful businessman she'd never seen. Wow...

The instant she looked, he looked back at her with dead accuracy, as if he knew exactly where she was at any given moment. He raised his glass a couple of inches in acknowledgement, and she reciprocated.

The rest of the room faded to white and his eyes seemed to drink her in. Warmth blossomed inside her. Was it the dress after all, she wondered, making her feel good? Or Steve's obvious appreciation back at the hotel when she'd exited her room?

'Anneliese? Anneliese Duffield?'

She turned her attention from Steve to the man at her side. Attractive guy, mid-forties. Great tan. 'Yes.'

'I'm Dan Stewart.' He offered his hand.

'Pleased to meet you, Dan. Are you one of Steve's clients?'

'I work for James Browning Industrial. A chartered accountant with the firm. Ever since Steve told us he was dating the famous Marcus Duffield's daughter, I've been looking forward to meeting you.'

'Oh?' she said vaguely as sensation slid down her spine. *Dating?* He'd told this man—more than this man apparently—that they were dating?

She flashed a look at Steve. At the broad shoulders, the way the light caught the sharp angle of his jaw. His killer smile as he spoke with clients. What would it be like to date Steve Anderson? To be the centre of his attention?

Until she remembered his attention span was notoriously short. 'When was this?' she asked Dan.

'This morning when we met.' He signalled a circulating waiter, swapped his empty glass for another drink. 'I know your father well. He performed heart surgery on my grandmother a few years ago when I was living in Melbourne. A great guy. Always talking about his Annie. I'm glad I finally got to meet her.' He perused her face, then nodded. 'You have his eyes.'

She stiffened. A few weeks ago, the comment would have made her smile. Tonight it made her sad. Bitter. Her fingers clenched around the stem of her glass. 'No. I don't.'

He paused, his smile disappearing. 'I apologise. I've offended you.'

'No. No, of course not.' Cursing herself, she blinked at him and summoned up a smile. Now that she thought about it, she did feel off—cold, shivery, but her skin was on fire. 'I skipped lunch, this cocktail must be going to my head. I meant—'

'Water's what you need.' He cupped her elbow and began steering her towards the long tables set along one wall where glass jugs had been set out, and poured her one.

'Thank you.'

'And some fresh air. Shall we find a seat outside away from the crowd for a bit?' He gestured to a set of glass doors. 'There's a courtyard through there.'

Dan set her down on the seat beneath a palm lit with fairy lights. 'I'll find out when the food's coming, see if I can rustle up something a little more substantial than poppadams and chips in the meantime.'

He studied her a moment, then dropped down on the seat beside her, frowning at her cheeks and then her shoulders. 'You're sunburnt. No wonder you're feeling out of sorts— you're dehydrated.' He patted her hand, then rose. 'I'll be back with—'

'Dan, isn't it?' Anneliese looked up at the sharp tone and saw Steve coming to a halt just outside the door.

He didn't move any closer, but his presence seemed to augment until Anneliese felt as if she were in the shadow of a mountain. A shadow, because she couldn't see the expression on his face, backlit as he was by the light spilling from the room behind him. The air, fragrant with tropical scents, hummed with the sudden tension and her fingers clenched around her glass.

'Yes.' Obviously Dan felt it, too, and took a step away. 'I was just telling Annie that her sunburn needs attention.'

'I don't doubt it.' Steve's words stabbed the air. 'She sunbathed today without protection. Isn't that right, Annie?'

She didn't miss the slightly mocking emphasis on her pet

name. 'I'm afraid so.' She smiled apologetically at Dan. 'I've just come from the end of winter down south.'

Steve knew he shouldn't have followed her, but he'd taken one look at the pair stepping outside and something inside him had erupted.

What he'd seen from the door had singed the edges of his control. The man's hand on Anneliese's. Too late he'd realised the innocent gesture for what it was. Concern. Concern that Steve himself might have shown if he'd taken better care. Damn it.

He willed his shoulders to relax as he walked towards them, fixing a smile on his face. 'Thanks, Dan, I'll see she gets the attention she needs.' He stepped to her and placed a hand on the small of her back, feeling her warmth through the fabric. 'Right now there's someone I want to introduce her to.'

'I'll let you get on with it.' Dan inclined his head to Anneliese. 'Great to meet you. Give your father my regards.'

She smiled. 'I will. Steve, what's the matter with you?' she muttered as Dan walked back inside.

Steve wasn't sure. One thing he did know was that he'd over-reacted. But that didn't stop him from saying, 'You seem to have made friends mighty fast,' as he steered her towards the door.

'If you're wondering why Dan referred to me as Annie, it's because he knows Dad. I only came out here bec—'

'It's not important.' He dismissed it with a shrug. 'I want you to meet...' His words trailed off as he slid his hand over her shoulders and felt a barely there shiver. He frowned at the heat he felt beneath his palm, then looked closer. 'You really are burned,' he murmured.

'Yes, I really am. And what do you mean, "it's not important"? You *really* are an arrogant man.'

Because she was right he clenched his jaw, then turned her towards him. 'I didn't mean that the way it sounded. A few introductions, then we'll leave and we can discuss it reasonably. When we're alone.'

Her hands went to her hips; her eyes flashed green fire. 'And how are you going to introduce me, Steve? Because Dan there is under the impression that we're *dating*.'

Steve felt his jaw drop in astonishment. 'I never said that.' But this whole scenario was beginning to feel as if they were. Memories of old arguments and hateful words scraped over his nerves.

'Why did Dan use that word, then? What's more, you dropped my father's name into the conversation. To drum up business, perhaps?'

He felt the sting in her voice, all the more powerful because she kept her voice low. Anger geysered up and his own voice was soft and dangerous when he leaned close and curled his fingers around her upper arms. 'I don't need your father's name to sell my business.' Remembering her sunburn, he loosened his hold a little but didn't release her. 'We'll go inside now and finish this conversation later.'

It was nearly 11:00 p.m. by the time they arrived back at Capricorn. He had to hand it to her, Anneliese could play a part. She'd won over his clients and their partners with sparkling and animated conversation. No one would have guessed at the tension between the two of them. No one except perhaps the helicopter pilot who flew them back to Surfers, or the limo driver who dropped them at the hotel.

They rode their private elevator side by side, eyes straight ahead. They entered the suite without a word. He slung his suit jacket on the nearest chair. When she crossed the floor to her bedroom, he broke the silence. 'Annie, I—'

'I know.' She turned, her eyes that intriguing blend of not quite blue, not quite green. 'I need to get out of this dress first—the straps are chafing.'

A damn shame. They might not be on speaking terms but he hadn't finished admiring her in it. He nodded, yanking off his tie. 'Okay. Do you want a drink?'

'Water. Please.'

Water wasn't going to do it for him tonight so he fixed himself a brandy on ice. Grabbing a tumbler, he opened the small fridge for cold water and saw a few salad vegetables Anneliese had obviously bought. He filled the tumbler, then, with Anneliese's sunburn in mind, he set about slicing cucumber thinly onto a plate.

He slid the door to the patio open and let the salty night air waft into the room while he replayed the evening's events and let the cool liquor slide down his throat. His clients were revved about his software designs and the viability of the product; everything was set to go. And Anneliese had fitted in so well by his side.

So he'd been told, several times. A success every way you looked at it, except that Anneliese wouldn't be there when they celebrated the job's completion.

Dan Stewart had assumed they were dating.

It had niggled at Steve the whole evening—the fact that the guy had used the word to Anneliese. Steve couldn't deny his developing feelings for her—had he, by his own words, by his very actions, propagated that idea?

How did Anneliese feel about Dan's choice of words? He tried to picture her expression when she'd told him what Dan had said, but all he could recall was that she'd been mad as hell and they'd both sniped at each other.

How would it feel to see Anneliese on a regular basis? Friends? Or lovers?

He didn't have time to ponder further because he heard her door close and turned to see her, her skin pink against a loose white jersey vest-top and shorts, reminding him again of coconut ice.

Something powerful twisted inside him. Was 'ice' going to be the operative word here? He didn't want to be frozen out by those eyes tonight. He needed warmth and companionship; he hadn't realised how much until this moment. He had no one close to share the success of the evening with except Anneliese and he desperately wanted it.

Friends or lovers?

He didn't look at those eyes. Instead, he gestured to the low glass table where he'd set her drink and sliced cucumber, then sat down and waited till she joined him on the plump leather sofa for two. She smelled so good. That fragrance was becoming an addiction.

He set his glass down. 'I shouldn't've—'

'I didn't mean what I—'

He glanced at her as they both spoke at the same time and found he couldn't drag his gaze away. Didn't want to. Her eyes were that soft blue-gum green. With arms that suddenly felt like lead weights he reached for her face, cupped it between his hands. 'Annie…' Her lips were pale pink, plump and lightly glossed and he leaned in to rub his own against them.

He intended the touch to be gentle—not even a kiss, rather a caress—but her lips parted softly, inviting him in. He licked at her tongue, then slid farther into the moist cavern of her mouth. She tasted of cream and cinnamon from the profiteroles she'd eaten, and a subtle deeper, richer flavour that seemed to seep into his blood. She was like finding sweet water in the middle of a desert.

Beneath his palms he could feel the pulse in her throat pounding beneath the delicate skin. His own pulse sky-rocketed as her hands, cool, smooth and sensual, came up to curl around his forearms, her fingernails tracing erotic circles on the inside of his wrists.

He felt himself floating, falling. He could go all the way…

With superhuman effort, he drew back, gazing into those beautiful slumberous eyes. 'I've wanted to do that all night.' All year. All my life.

She blinked. 'I'm not your type. You're not mine. And yet…' She blinked again. He'd never been turned on by a blink before, but he was now.

'And yet…?' he murmured, his lips a whisper away from hers. He hadn't known how much he wanted to hear her say it.

But her hands rose to touch her mouth and he stifled his disappointment.

'We're alike in some ways, you and I,' he said. 'Wealth brings problems. Sometimes it attracts the wrong people.'

She shook her head. 'I shouldn't have accused you of using my father's name.'

But he wasn't thinking of that. He was remembering a woman called Caitlyn, and he hated the thought of Anneliese being used for her family's wealth the way he had, which went some way to explain his actions where Dan was concerned, since Dan knew she came from money.

'What say we put the evening behind us?' He reached for the cucumber slices and patted the sofa. 'Lie down and let me ease your sunburn with something cool.'

She glanced at the plate and smiled as she said, 'And here I was thinking you were trying to seduce me with food.'

He heard the hitch in her voice, saw the flash of realisation in her eyes the instant the words left her mouth. *Don't tempt me.* He kept his voice teasing and said, 'If I wanted to seduce you with food, I'd go for something more classy than sliced cucumber.'

Biting her lip, she swung her legs, those stunningly long legs, along the sofa.

'Close your eyes.' He placed slices on her cheeks, her brow, one on each of her eyelids, on her *décolletage*… His hand hovered over her thighs. Where the loose jersey afforded glimpses of forbidden territory. There wasn't nearly enough cucumber, and he really didn't think this was a good idea after all...

'I'll call room service and get some sunburn lotion sent up.'

She waved a hand. 'No, I have lotion in my room. I didn't want to smell like suncream all evening. To satisfy a curiosity,' she said slowly, as if deep in thought, 'how *would* you go about seducing someone?'

For a few stunned seconds he stared at her. Her eyes remained hidden behind the cucumber mask. 'I don't seduce women,' he said quietly. 'At least not the way I think you mean. It's a mutual decision based on respect.'

He watched her bottom lip pout before she closed her teeth over it and he clenched his jaw as heat jiggered through his body. He wanted to kiss her again but danger lurked down that road. 'Annie...' He peeled the cucumber slices from her eyes, searching her gaze.

It struck like a blow. Why she'd always acted so skittish around him, why she froze him out. She'd wanted him, even three years back. The way he wanted her.

All the way.

And right now that was too damn complicated. 'We're friends,' he murmured. 'You said so yourself.'

'What if...?'

What if we became lovers? He pushed the thought away. 'How about a night on the town tomorrow night? We've never enjoyed an evening together, just the two of us. Let's make it supper.'

'Like a date?'

She looked so young and appealing, her sun-kissed cheeks glowing, her eyes wide with expectation, he gave in. 'Okay. Call it a date.'

And this time her smile really did reach her eyes. *Hallelujah!* He pushed off the sofa before he said—or did—something he might regret. Like leaning over and kissing her senseless. 'I need some shut-eye. Be ready at 9:00 p.m.'

CHAPTER TEN

ANNELIESE stared at her reflection in the mirror. The dress was so…vivid. She'd never worn red before. The shiny material—what there was of it—clung to her body, dipping low between her breasts showing off her sparkly diamond and ruby necklace. She turned around to view the back, which was almost non-existent. Spaghetti-thin straps held the whole thing together. It matched her skin, she thought with a final wry glance over her shoulder.

'You chose red for a reason,' she told her reflection. *Here I am—I'm taking action now. Watch out, Steve, here I come.* No pastels tonight. She'd had all day to think about it. He wanted her. Those heated looks he'd been giving her. The times she'd caught him watching her. Why else would he have kissed her again last night even when she'd pulled away from him that morning in her apartment?

And last night with Dan… She'd replayed the scene in her head over and over. Steve hadn't been angry so much as jealous, she was sure of it.

Lord knew, she wanted him. She'd wanted him for years. Only now was she able to come to terms with the fact. Instead of retreating behind the façade she'd hidden behind for so long it had become second nature, she was stepping out. Life had a funny way of kicking you up the bum when you least expected it. Her family was a lie. She had a sister she was about to meet. Who knew what might happen tomorrow?

Tonight if he didn't seduce her... She shook away the thought. This was Steve Anderson, 'playboy of the year' contender.

For a moment her excitement ebbed. Guys like Steve didn't stay focused for long. Eyeballing herself, she fluffed her hair in defiance. It didn't matter. Perhaps it was as they said, an itch. Maybe if they made love she'd get it out of her system. For now she refused to think beyond the evening—

'Good evening, Annie.'

She hadn't heard the door open, and saw his reflection before the real thing. Her hands stilled on her thighs. He stood a metre or so behind her holding a single long-stemmed rose the colour of flushed porcelain. The air around her was suddenly thick with that familiar tension and her legs felt weak and she couldn't breathe—it was like old times. *Pull yourself together.*

'Hi,' she said to his reflection, and imagined the suit and shirt and blue tie melting off his body. He'd had his hair cut, she noticed, still looking in the mirror. A shorter style but it still had that messy look, as if he'd just rolled out of bed.

He couldn't seem to take his eyes off her dress and with the mirror he had a good view of both front and back. Her face felt hot. And not only her face—was he imagining her naked?

'W-o-w. Fire-engine red.' His gaze smouldered as it slid from her stiletto-clad feet to mid-calf where the dress began, then up over the fabric, singeing all her important places until finally he met her eyes. She shivered in the aftermath.

'I always thought pastel colours suited you.' His voice sounded charred as he held out the rose. 'Perhaps I should have gone with the red bud after all. Which reminds me, how's the sunburn?'

'Getting better. And, no, this is beautiful. My favourite colour.' She lifted it to her nose to breathe in its scent and feel the velvet texture against her face. 'Thank you.'

When he leaned in to drop a kiss on her cheek, she turned her head at the last minute and met his mouth. For a moment she couldn't feel any part of her body beyond the warm touch of his lips as they pressed against hers. The taste of peppermint and something salty as their tongues collided.

This is what I've been waiting for my whole life, she thought and leaned in to deepen the kiss. Right now she wanted him more than any dinner. She couldn't help but wonder that she'd known him for years and hadn't recognised what she'd wanted. This man. His friendship, support and understanding. And— fingers crossed—tonight, something more. In a bold move, she slid her hands over his shirt, feeling the rock-hard muscle beneath.

'Whoa,' he said softly, grasping her hands, and lifting his head to look at her. 'Where's the fire?'

'In this dress, you're asking me?' She almost choked, almost laughed. Where had that sultry voice come from?

His grin faded almost as soon as it appeared, as if he'd suddenly remembered who she was. 'Come on,' he said, stepping back. 'I've booked something I hope you'll like.'

It took forty seconds to reach the Q1's Skylight Room on the seventy-eighth floor. Anneliese didn't know whether the dizzy feeling was caused by the lift or being on a date with Steve.

When the lift doors slid open, revealing a dimly lit room, Anneliese whispered, 'Are we too late?'

'No. We're right on time. Tonight's just for us.'

'You booked the whole room?' *Was there no end to the magic?* she wondered as they were met by staff and shown to a table already set for two. And it was dim because the soft glow of a multitude of candles was the only source of light.

The scent of tropical flowers wafted to her nostrils as she took her seat, absorbing the glorious view of the lights spread out below like a jewelled black carpet with its rippled fringe of coast and sea.

Lifting the rose's velvet petals to her nose, she turned her admiring gaze from the view to the man. The city's lights threw up a subtle glow and joined with the candles to reflect in his eyes. She gave over to the pleasure of watching his face. Seeing his own pleasure in the way his eyes crinkled, in the curve of his lips. 'Nobody's ever done anything like this for me. Thank you.'

'I selected the menu, so I hope you enjoy it.' He withdrew a chilled bottle from the ice bucket beside him. '*Voilà.*'

She clasped her hands in delight. 'French champagne.'

A waiter stepped forward to pop the cork and pour.

Another waiter placed a selection of seafood—prawns, oysters Kilpatrick, crayfish, smoked salmon on a salad of rocket leaves, baby tomatoes, capers and lemon wedges.

'I know you like seafood.' He shelled a prawn and dipped it in sauce, held it out to her.

She took it between her lips and chewed, her eyes on his as he peeled his own, popped it into his mouth. 'Divine.'

'Indeed,' he agreed. He handed her a flute of bubbly and raised his own. '*Que sera sera*, Annie.' He clinked it to hers.

Anneliese took a long slow swallow of champagne. Bubbles danced in her nose and fizzed down her throat while she tried to interpret what he meant by *what will be will be*. 'You're a believer in fate, then?'

'Only *you* can make your own happiness, so *que sera sera*'s what you make of it.' He set down his glass and selected an oyster. 'Tell me about the girl who rescues animals.'

'Hasn't Cindy ever told you?'

His mouth turned down ever so slightly at the corners.

'Cindy doesn't have a lot to say to me. I'm only her annoying big brother. Who's still getting used to the idea that she's been an adult for quite a while.'

'She may not say it, but she thinks the world of you. You've always been there for her, like her dad used to be. You'll make someone a great dad yourself some day.'

Instantly his eyes clouded, his lips compressed and he shifted inside his shirt. Almost a first to see him not entirely comfortable in his own skin.

'Don't you want children of your own down the track?'

'No.' Cold, flat, non-negotiable. 'Family life's not for me.'

Even the air temperature around them seemed to drop and she shivered as she stared at his thin-lipped denial. The sadness, its emptiness, echoed like tears on her own lost soul. This man had been hurt.

Because of his mother? She knew the woman had walked out on her children years ago. The way her biological mother had abandoned her. Because children were too much damn trouble.

She reached out and touched his hand. 'You're not only Cindy's brother, you're her hero.'

He drew a circle on the tablecloth with a finger, then looked up, dark, haunted eyes meeting hers for a scant second before skidding to the view below. 'I'm sure she'll be thrilled with you for sharing that.'

As if sweeping the thought away, he straightened, his expression clearing. 'You were going to tell me about your work.'

'I've been working in a voluntary capacity at an animal shelter and adoption agency for the past few years. You mentioned veterinary science to me once. I still want to study it some day.'

'What's preventing you from starting now?'

'Mum says... Mum *said*...' Guilt skulked on the edge of her conscience and she had to take a breath. Now she was free to do what she'd wanted to do for years.

Because her mother was gone.

'You okay?' His hand covered hers.

'Fine.'

He squeezed her hand. 'It'll get better with time.'

She nodded, took another deep breath. 'I think I'll look into it when I go back.'

They ate, they drank, and watched a shower of rain turn the view into water-colour reflections. They shared the raspberry and rosewater clafoutis dessert and listened to a flute and guitar duo Steve had organised to serenade them.

At the moment the musicians were playing something fast and passionate and Spanish. Steve watched Anneliese, her eyes misty, lost in the world of music. Unable to resist, he let the knuckles of one hand drift over her smooth rosy cheek. He'd never felt the urge to touch a woman the way he wanted to touch Anneliese. Constantly.

She turned those misty green eyes on him—he was discovering they turned greener when she was happy, blue when sad or angry—and he wanted to forget he couldn't take it further. He wanted to forget everything except taking her back to her room, his room—any room—and making love to her till neither of them could move. But this fast-tempo music was the nearest thing to passion coming his way tonight. Or any other night.

A short time later the band packed up and the waiter delivered their coffee and asked if there was anything else before he left them to their privacy.

He watched Anneliese's lips glisten as she took a slow sip of the strong black coffee, and yanked down his tie, which was suddenly strangling him. Why had he thought this a good idea?

She picked up the delicate pink rose. 'Thank you for a lovely evening.'

He watched her stroke the petals over her chin. He wanted to perform that sensual task. And he wouldn't stop at the chin… His eyes drifted down over the globes of her breasts before lifting again to hers—green as spring grass. 'You've always reminded me of a rose,' he said. 'Tall, slender, prickly, a joy to look at.'

He wanted to kiss her. Now, with candle-flame flickering on her face and her lips curved into a smile. His own lips tingled. Other parts of his body joined in. 'I'd like to see you in moonlight,' he murmured. *Wearing nothing but moonbeams.* 'Or firelight.'

Her eyes darkened as she lifted a brow. 'One's cool, one's hot.' The tip of her tongue flicked the corner of her mouth, probably innocent but no less provocative.

'Moonlight, then,' he said. 'It suits you. Cool, classical, ethereal.'

His body wasn't paying attention to the words. Heat flared in his groin, burned in his veins. His eyes slid over her red dress and he couldn't help imagining how he'd go about taking it off. He'd take his time, slow and lazy, make it last. A few skinny straps to ease over her shoulders, then just the whisper of his hands on hot silk and satin skin…

'You're so damn beautiful,' he murmured. He combed her hair behind her ears with his fingers, then cupped her face, letting his fingers enjoy the texture of her skin—soft on her cheeks, smooth along her brow, warm beneath her jaw.

And he groaned as he finally gave in to the pleasure and gently savoured the sweet taste of her mouth. She reciprocated with a murmured whimpering sound that sang through his blood.

How could he resist? This was like an addiction. A torture because there was no satisfying this craving. This kiss, this perfect kiss that invited all sorts of lush temptations…

He pulled back. Before he was ready. Her gaze met his and

he was shocked to find how much he wanted *not* to let her go. He wanted to kiss her again but it felt terrifyingly more like need than desire, and he never wanted to need again.

Her smile was something he was going to see over and over in his sleep. Was it possible to play casual with Anneliese? After all the years of wanting and wondering, she was within his grasp. Literally and figuratively. She wanted him. Why not take it to the next step?

Because he'd taken on a responsibility. He had to keep her safe, and that included keeping her safe from himself.

He tugged her lacy black wrap from the back of her chair and handed it to her. 'It's time to go.'

Anneliese slipped off her wrap the moment they entered the suite. Steve had been quiet all the way back. She watched him shrug out of his suit jacket, undo his cuffs. Watched the sinews twist in his forearms as he rolled up his sleeves, revealing dark masculine hair. She wanted those arms around her.

'Would you like another coffee?' she asked, twirling Steve's rose between her fingers.

'No, thanks.' He picked up the TV remote and flicked through the channels till he found one with car racing, then sat on the sofa, eyes glued to the screen.

Her own eyes were glued to the back of his head. After a wonderful date—he'd thought of everything, from the limo ride, to the location on the top of the world, the romantic music to the simple rose—he'd opted to watch TV sports.

She lifted the bloom to her nose. He'd called her beautiful. He'd kissed her as if there were no tomorrow. And now he was watching TV. What did that mean? The man was a playboy, he *liked* women, he liked sleeping with them—if he got any sleep, that was. And she didn't want to think about that. Why wasn't he making a move on her now?

He must have felt the daggers in his skull because he glanced around and their eyes met. A loaded silence ensued. She could hear the sea through the patio doors, the sounds of traffic. The echo of her own heartbeat. Without taking his eyes from hers he found the off button and the TV screen went dark. Anticipation shivered over her skin as he walked towards her. Her nipples hardened beneath the silk.

His eyes remained on hers with every step he took. When he reached her, he bent his head, the scent of his skin teasing her nostrils. Without touching any other body part, he gently, almost reverently kissed her lips. And then he said, 'I think I'll call it a night. Sleep well, princess.'

'I…' Numb, she continued to stand where she was for several minutes, staring sightlessly at the view beyond the balcony. She dropped the rose on the coffee-table to rub a hand across her chest in a futile effort to slow the beat of her runaway heart. Had she assumed wrongly all along that he wanted her? *No*.

Yet just when she'd thought he was going to take her hand and lead her to his room, he'd bid her goodnight. That didn't make sense—he was, after all, a ladies' man.

She frowned. She was a lady. Maybe not his kind of lady, but that was what she wanted to know about. What was *wrong* with her? Did she have *virgin* stamped on her forehead? Was inexperience a turn-off for him? Spinning around on her heel, she headed for his room.

She set her palm on his door and pushed gently. It swung open soundlessly on a soft draught of air tinged with Steve's aftershave.

She froze, staring while her pulse leapt to renewed life. Oh, my goodness… He'd taken off his shirt and was standing by the bed stabbing numbers into his mobile, oblivious to her. His upper body gleamed in the light and was dusted with dark hair that arrowed south… She bit down on her lip. He'd also stripped off his belt and undone the top button of his trousers.

Dimly, it registered that she'd never seen his body shirtless before. Bronze and perfectly sculptured, as if he'd been modelled on an ancient Greek statue.

Her eyes couldn't seem to look away and she remained rooted to the spot in an agony of indecision. Any movement might alert him to the fact that she was watching him unannounced. Uninvited. Unnerved. If she could just back away slowly…

He set his mobile on the night-stand, raked his hands through his hair, then reached for his zipper—

'Steve!' The urgent plea sounded like a gunshot in the silence.

His eyes flicked to the doorway. He paused in his task. 'Annie.' Surprise gave way to a frown. 'Something wrong?'

'Umm.' She found she could move after all and wrung her hands, finding them damp and limp. 'I'm sorry. To…catch you…' she waved one of those limp hands towards his chest '…like that.'

'Is something wrong?' he asked again.

'No. I mean yes.'

'Come in, Annie.' He reached for his shirt, shrugged into it again, but left it undone. His hair was furrowed, the shirt hem was creased and the whole look screamed disreputable. He looked at her as he sat down and patted the luxury blue quilt. 'Sit yourself down here and tell me the problem.'

Stepping out of her shoes, she crossed the room and perched on the edge of the bed. Now she was here and completely overwhelmed by his pure physicality and didn't know how to say what she'd come to say. Her mouth was dry and she wished the glass of water on his night-stand were within reach.

'You're the problem,' she said, and forced herself to look at him.

His brows puckered. 'What have I done?'

'It's what you haven't done.'

'Okay,' he said slowly. 'What haven't I done?'

She looked down at her hands clenched together on her red satin dress and tried to ignore the sting of heat rising up her neck. If she didn't say it, she'd always regret it. 'You… I see it in your eyes…and I know you know how I feel. You kiss me as if you mean it, then everything comes to a halt. You've never tried to…' She looked up at him again, seeing the incredulous expression—as if the idea were preposterous.

'Are you kidding?' A harsh laugh escaped his lips as he shook his head, then raked a hand through his hair, leaving it more tousled than ever. He jerked off the bed and paced to the window.

Humiliation washed over her like hot acid. She'd been wrong; she'd never been more wrong. How was she ever going to face him? 'Never try to kiss me again.' She dragged herself up and was halfway across the room when he snagged her arm.

'You've got it all wrong.' His dark eyes flashed like black diamonds; his mouth was a hard line in an uncompromising face. 'Why the hell do you think I kissed you in the first place?' He tugged her back to the bed and pressed her down, knelt before her, cupped her face in his hands. 'Don't you know? I like you, Annie. I like you a lot. Too damn much to spoil what we have with a cheap affair.' He ground out the words as if he were chewing leather. 'I shouldn't have kissed you.' Then he closed his eyes for a brief moment. 'Hell.'

Her heart wouldn't stop pounding; it was pounding its way up her throat and into her mouth. 'Why not?'

'Because it makes things complicated. We're surrounded by holiday-makers in an idyllic setting.' He waved a hand at the room. 'This luxury hotel. Surfers Paradise is a tourist trap—it's easy to be caught up in it.'

'So, you're saying when we go home it all just fades away?'

'Yes. No. I don't know.' He shook his head. 'Make no mistake, I want you, Annie, but more important: the last thing I want to do is hurt you.' Then the words she'd been half expecting: 'I don't do long term.'

'What if I don't want long term?'

'Take it from me, and I speak from experience, a girl like you wants long term.'

'A girl like me?' Who knew what kind of family she'd been born into before she'd been adopted? 'There's a lot you don't know about me, Steve.'

He inclined his head in a gesture of acknowledgement. His hands slid away from her face and he leaned back on his heels. 'Think very carefully about what you want. Wishes are pretty things, but they have an ugly habit of coming back to bite you.'

He rose, turned his back on her and stalked to the open door that led to his balcony. She watched him step out, watched the breeze catch at his shirt tails and riffle his hair. Heaven help her, she was falling in love with him. Without another word, she rose, too, and left him to his own thoughts, knowing this conversation, at least, was over.

CHAPTER ELEVEN

THE tension between them increased over the next couple of days. Steve was forced to change his earlier assessment that Anneliese was easy to read. Last night she'd gone to her room early after they'd shared a meal in their suite. To do what, he didn't know. To think about last night's conversation? To avoid him? He felt as if he were sitting on a knife's edge awaiting some sort of decision. He'd made it clear he wanted her. He'd also made it clear he didn't want to hurt her.

This evening she was metres away from him on the sofa watching TV. Steve was busy on his computer concentrating on figures that wouldn't compute. He wished it were her figure he was concentrating on. That his fingers were working over the dips and curves of her body rather than the unresponsive keys on his laptop. His skin tightened with heat despite the cool breeze blowing off the ocean and into their apartment. The task would demand the same all-consuming attention and be a hell of a lot more pleasurable.

But he refused to look up, even when she sighed in that breathy little way that reminded him of how she sounded when he kissed her soft, sweet mouth. How would she sound if he pleasured her in other sweet places? *No.* He'd left the choice up to her, he wasn't going to influence her.

Uncurling her slim body, she rose and stretched. Her vest-top strained against perfect female flesh—not that he was looking—then she walked to the fridge, her brief jersey shorts giving him an eyeful of long smooth leg. Her sunburn had faded somewhat, leaving her skin a pale gold. He forced his gaze back to the screen, but his burgeoning desire took precedence over the complex diagrams of the security system he was supposed to be refining.

'Fancy a slice of mango?' she asked.

He glanced up to see her holding a knife and a bowl of chilled fruit against her breasts. Was she baiting him? His eyes flicked to hers but he saw no guile in those clear green eyes. Without conscious thought he let his gaze slide lower. Her *décolletage* glowed with a thin film of sweat and, with her in that skinny black souvenir top that boasted a Hot Night in Paradise with its stylised hot pink lips, he knew what he fancied and it wasn't the mango. 'No. Thank you.'

But he could've done with some of its cool relief to douse the fire burning in his loins. The air felt hot and oppressive with the threat of a thunderstorm. Somewhere down the street he could hear the thump of bass, the fast beat of dance music. People, he thought. Lots of people. Distraction.

He clicked off his laptop, snapped it shut. 'Annie, put on something nice and we'll go out.'

'Out?' He thought he saw a flash of—was it surprise or anticipation?—in her eyes.

'Yeah.' He forced a casual tone to his voice. 'We haven't hit any of the night-spots yet. There's a trendy place about twenty minutes' walk away.'

'I'll need to shower and change and—'

'Fine. I'll do the same. Meet you back here when you're done.'

When she appeared thirty minutes later in a white crushed-silk dress and looking a cool million dollars with her diamond and ruby necklace circling her slender neck, he wondered if he'd made the right decision in suggesting they go out after all.

'Let's get going, then,' he said in that same casual voice, and, forcing his eyes away from the sight, he headed for the door.

He wasn't the only one looking at Anneliese, he noticed as they crossed the lobby. A couple of staff at the concierge desk tracked their progress to the glass doors. Almost as if they recognised her. He gave a mental shrug, but sidled closer and caught her fingers. An unconsciously possessive move, he realised, but he didn't release her. They'd probably seen her coming and going and were as taken in by her stunning looks as he.

They exited the building and stepped into a muggy evening filled with tourists. The sea was a soft sibilance of background sound against muffled music, idle chatter and the hum of traffic. The air, heavy with the smell of salt and hot food, clung to his skin already damp with humidity. Anneliese's palm was soft and cool against his and he firmed his grip. It felt right at home there. What was more, she didn't pull away.

Which left him wondering… What was she thinking? What had she decided? He turned his attention to the here and now as they walked past yet another luxury tower and tugged her hand. 'Let's walk on the other side of the road.'

'Where are we heading to?'

'Orchard Avenue. I heard about a spot where the music's more important than the liquor.' And that was what he wanted. A place to give his body the workout he'd put on hold over the last few days.

'But don't we need to head away from the esplanade and go—'

'We're taking the scenic route.'

'Okay…' she said slowly. 'Is it just music, or is there dancing?'

'Both. Do you like to dance?'

'I do. You?'

'Yeah, when— Did you feel that?'

At his abrupt change in tone Anneliese jerked her thoughts from imagining Steve holding her in a slow waltz to the cupped hand he held out in front of him. The other hand was clasped around hers. Amazing. A few days ago that simple touch would have set alarm bells ringing. Tonight it just felt…right. 'Feel what?'

'I think we're in for some rain.'

She glanced up and noticed the clouds for the first time, their heavy underbellies glowing pink with reflected light. Then felt the first large plops hit her face and bare arms.

'Uh, oh. Come on,' he said, tugging her hand. 'We'll take shelter on the other side of the road.'

'No. Wait.' Even as she slipped off her stilettos, the plops turned to buckets, scattering tourists to the closest shelters. The scent of wet cement and coastal vegetation rose up to meet her. Car tyres swished water over the road. 'To that tree,' she called, yanking her hand from his and heading for the nearest Norfolk Island Pine on the esplanade.

Norfolk Island Pines, she discovered, when they got there, weren't going to offer much shelter from this downpour. She was soaked to the skin, water sluicing over her face and dripping between her breasts. The rain turned the air around the lights misty, so the whole world was bathed in a golden glow.

Dropping her purse and shoes, she leaned back against the trunk and swiped at the hair plastered wetly to her cheeks. The expensive dry-clean-only silk was probably ruined. No doubt she had panda eyes from smeared mascara. And she'd never felt so free. She laughed, lifting her eyes to Steve's.

Rain coursed down the grooves bracketing his nose and

mouth and gleamed on his face. It glittered like tiny jewels on the hair sprouting over his V-neck sweater and clung to his thick eyelashes.

And the laugh faded.

His gaze was dark velvet, reaching inside her, warming the lonely place in her soul that she'd never allowed herself to acknowledge existed, let alone explore. Tonight she saluted it, welcomed it. Embraced it.

She could smell his skin, warm and musky and wet with the fragrant moisture of clean rain. Could feel his need, fingers of heat stroking her skin as he stepped closer, shielding her from the downpour and trapping her against the tree—almost—because no part of his body yet touched hers.

His breath whisked over her cheeks. He was going to kiss her, and how she'd missed it. She raised her face to his, the reflection of a thousand twinkling lights in those dark eyes as anticipation drummed through her veins like the storm.

Her eyelids slid shut. Drawing a deep breath, she held it, lips tingling, waiting for that first touch...

Nothing.

Her eyes blinked open. He was still there, his mouth scant millimetres away from hers, his hair dripping water onto her face. 'What?' she whispered.

'Are you sure?'

She didn't answer, just inched her body closer, letting the anticipation build, until the tips of her breasts grazed his chest, until she felt the hard, hot length of his body against hers. Then she slid her arms around his waist, splayed her hands over his back and clung.

Warm hands cupped her face. 'Annie.'

Without waiting she reached up and touched her lips to his. Warm, sweet and wet with rain. She drank him in, opening her mouth to him and letting his flavour linger on her tongue.

In the distance a nightclub was belting out a heavy bass track, to her left she could hear the *shoosh* of the surf. But they faded to the sound of her heart beating in her ears.

Damp denim chafed her legs and the short skirt of her dress as with a subtle movement he shifted closer, manoeuvring her back against the prickly bark. She lifted a leg to wrap it around one hard calf, to arch her instep and rub it along the denim. And then she felt the full force of his erection pressed against her belly. *Oh, my…goodness.*

Her eyes jerked open as the impact of what she was doing sank in. She was still rubbing up against…Steve Anderson. And Steve Anderson was still rubbing up against her…

On a public street in the middle of Surfers. What was happening to her? Was she out of her mind? Yes, she decided, she probably was.

He lifted his lips a fraction to murmur, 'Relax,' but she took the opportunity to slip out from his grasp. She grabbed her shoes and purse, turned back and began running towards the hotel.

Seconds later he was right there with her. 'Hey,' he said. 'Annie. It's okay.'

'I…know,' she said between breaths, feeling a surge of something beyond anything she'd ever felt in her life. 'I… mean…it's *really*…okay.'

She didn't stop when they reached the lobby, but she did slow to a walk. Barely. She murmured an apology to any staff within hearing as they trailed water over the gleaming floor, and kept going. Out to the patio where the aquamarine pool glittered with underwater lighting. She dropped her shoes and purse by the shallow edge of the pool, and jumped in feet first.

Cool water sucked the heat from her body as she surfaced, slicking her hair from her eyes and searching for Steve. 'Yes!' she shouted when she saw him on the edge of the pool poised to jump. 'Yes, yes and yes!'

He was beside her in one almighty splash. 'Yes, what, Annie?'

'Yes. I'm sure.'

Strong arms slid around her waist. 'I think...' he rubbed his lips over hers '...we're disturbing the guests.'

She snuck a peek and saw one of the staff approaching. The few guests lingering beneath the shelter with their late drinks stared. She slicked her hair back again, since he'd half drowned her when he'd jumped, and looked up at him. The water lapped coolly at her shoulders.

'I'm aware of that,' she said primly. He bumped up hard against her as they disentangled their legs and stood. 'And I'm aware of *that*.' She knew he knew what she was referring to. And the implications. 'The answer's still yes.'

So what if it wasn't permanent? She wanted this. Wanted him. She wasn't so naïve that she didn't know his reputation with women. That this was Surfers and when they went home everything would change. She was making a decision, on her own, with her eyes wide open.

'Excuse me, sir, madam, but I'll have to ask you to leave the pool.'

'I apologise,' Steve said to the anxious staff member awaiting them with thick fluffy towels when they clambered out.

'Sorry...' Anneliese mentally frowned at the staff member's expression as he stared at her, backing away as if he'd seen a ghost.

But he was forgotten as Steve shook out the first towel, draped it over Anneliese, then began patting it over her drenched clothes. All over... Their eyes met and she wondered how the water didn't turn to steam. He shook his head, gave the ends of her towel into her hands and wrapped himself in the other. 'I think we're creating a scene here.'

Their first sanctuary, the private elevator to the first-floor Pisces Suite, was all gold fixtures, aqua-glazed mirrors and purple light, as befitting a marine theme. Even the floor and ceiling were mirrored. The soothing sounds of an underwater world bubbled through hidden speakers.

Anneliese leaned her head back against the wall and gazed up at their reflections on the ceiling. The sight jolted her. Was that half-drowned woman letting Steve Anderson put his hands on her backside and nibble at her throat really Anneliese Duffield?

Maybe not, she thought. Maybe that was Hayley. Perhaps she'd taken on another personality. Because Anneliese Duffield would *not* be arching her neck and letting him take little nips along her collar-bone, her ear, her chin… Enjoying the feel of his lips and the way his stubble rasped over her skin.

At her sigh, he followed her gaze and their eyes met in the overhead mirror. Bathed in an almost ultra-violet light, the whole scene was surreal. Her white dress shimmered like opal, her arms and face glowed a sexy bronze.

Like Steve… His skin still looked so dark against hers, his eyes obsidian and intense. Potent. With his hair slicked back and dripping onto his shoulders, the strong jaw and sharp angles of his face, he looked more like a captor than a would-be lover.

Lover. The word slammed into her chest. And that was what he'd be. If that was what she wanted. She still had that choice, Steve had given it to her, and she could still change her mind…

Then the elevator door slid open, revealing the lobby to their suite's double door and cool light cascaded in. He didn't move. Neither did she, her gaze fixed on the view of the two of them above.

The moment of choice.

A few seconds later she heard the door slide shut again.

CHAPTER TWELVE

STEVE stepped away, but only to lock the lift in place. The significance of that action, the flash of heat—and intent—in his dark eyes, registered in Anneliese's euphoria-induced brain.

Still holding her gaze, he reached out to touch her. She held her breath as he slipped the camisole from her shoulders, down her arms, his fingers touching hers as he let it fall to the floor.

'Silk,' he murmured, and traced her arms again, upwards this time, the pads of his fingers creating such a delicate friction she felt as fragile as glass. 'Like your skin. I love your skin.' He trailed an open mouth over every inch of her shoulders, first one, then the other, sucking, licking and nipping and showing her without a doubt just how much he loved it.

Reaching behind her, he slid the zip of her dress down her back, the sound erotic in itself, his knuckles grazing every vertebra in another of those slow, delicate passes. Peeled the wet fabric from her body, his hands sliding down her arms, her torso, her thighs as he inched it lower, until it pooled at her feet.

His eyes dropped to her right side, near her hip. 'This is a surprise.'

She shivered as he trailed a finger of rippling pleasure over the taboo tattoo she'd had done for her eighteenth birthday. Three Chinese characters. Her little rebellion.

'It's a secret.' Her cheeks heated as the flush rose from her neck. Until this moment, no living soul apart from the tattoo artist had ever seen it.

'What does it say?'

'Body, mind and spirit.'

She watched the appreciation light his eyes as his gaze took in the rest of her. Her whole body felt as if it glowed from within. No one had ever looked at her this way.

No one had ever seen her this way.

The knowledge frightened her for a moment, but only for a moment because Steve was so gentle, so attentive. So caring. Her fear melted away in the warmth and security of their under-watery world…and Steve's strong and solid presence. She knew she was safe with him, knew by the way he looked into her eyes with the same gentleness and care he lavished on her body that if she changed her mind he'd respect that.

He cupped her breasts, testing their weight in his palms, and bent his head. And she felt herself go boneless. Her breath sighed out as he closed a hot mouth over one bra-covered nipple, then the other, suckling her through the white satin. 'Steve…' Her own hands came up of their own accord to stroke his damp hair and pull him closer, or perhaps it was to balance herself in a world that was starting to spin away.

He pulled back and she wanted to whimper at the loss. 'Annie,' he murmured and straightened. His eyes once again locked with hers.

He reached behind her again, his fingers deft and experienced as he unclipped her bra, drew the garment away and let it fall. Then his hands were on her hips, inside the straps that held the only scrap of lace protection left to her. Once more, his hands barely touched as he tugged her panties down to join her dress at her feet. Stepping away, she swept the unnecessary garments to one side with her foot.

All he left were the jewels glittering at her throat, the rubies black in the blue light, the diamonds catching greens and blues as she sucked in air in a suddenly airless space.

Only then did his gaze leave hers to look at what he'd uncovered. A slow and thorough perusal with those dark eyes that seemed to slide over her body like melted chocolate. 'My God, you're beautiful,' he breathed. He lifted her necklace, rubbed the central stone between his fingers. 'Rubies suit you. Red, for your hair. I love looking at you.' His lips curved. 'Princess Annie.'

She should have felt exposed and vulnerable, standing naked before a man for the first time, but she felt neither. Just warm and appreciated and…thoroughly turned on. It was as if he'd flicked some sort of erotic switch.

Through a red haze of desire she watched as he yanked off his sodden sweater, exposing the hard-packed chest with its sprinkle of dark hair and flat nipples. In the mirror behind him, she saw a broad, smooth back, the muscles bunched at his shoulders as he hitched at the waistband of his jeans.

Soaked jeans that hung low on his hips and now looked excruciatingly tight and distended at the front. Intoxication might have had something to do with the way she reached out to undo the stud, except she hadn't had a drink. Her hand grazed his hard ridge of arousal. She almost stopped breathing at that first brief contact. Her galloping pulse seemed to be centred in the tips of her fingers. Or perhaps it was his pulse; she couldn't be sure, but he didn't give her time to find out.

He sucked in a harsh breath. 'Not yet.' Grabbing her hand, he removed it from the front of his jeans, twining his fingers through hers, pressing both against the glass behind them. 'I want to see you. All of you.'

He laid his lips on hers for one brief but infinitely gentle moment. Then he stepped back, disentangled their fingers so that he could explore her naked body with hands and eyes. Slowly. Surely. As if he already knew every aching centimetre, as if he knew just where to touch to send her soaring to the beyond.

As his fingertips explored the shape of her breasts, the curve of her waist, the indentation of her navel, she refused to think about the other women, the fact that she was one in an endless string. For now he wanted her and that was enough.

When his hands slid over the tops of her thighs she collapsed back against the cool glass, closing her eyes, her hands clenching and unclenching at her sides. She could no longer feel her feet—or anywhere else, for that matter. Her entire focus was centred on one place. Wherever Steve touched.

He coaxed her legs apart with warm fingers. His other hand clamped onto one buttock. Heat spun through that already damp and untouched place and coiled low in her abdomen and she arched instinctively against his hand to ease the tension there.

He responded by drawing a finger, just once, over her slick centre. Her eyes snapped open and she gasped, spreading her legs wider, groping for his shoulders to anchor herself, her body reaching for a mysterious something she'd never experienced. She could smell the heat of his body, inches from hers, a mix of musky male overlaying the tang of the pool's chlorine.

Then she made the mistake of following his downward gaze to the mirrored floor beneath them. At the dark skin of his hand covering her pale flesh. Flesh that had never seen the light of day.

Now she was embarrassed. And raw and open and exposed. Her face and neck blossomed with a raging heat and the lovely feeling faded. She clamped her thighs together, but only succeeding in trapping him there.

He removed his hand from her backside, tilted her chin up

so she had no choice but to look at him, and stared into her eyes. 'Don't. Don't hide yourself. You're the most beautiful girl I ever saw, Annie. Everywhere.'

He eased her legs apart again and stroked her. Hot, sleek fingers sliding over and over and the delicious tension increased. Forget about being shy; she wanted to go wherever it was he was taking her. He pressed an open mouth to hers again. She moaned into it with pure greed, tasting him as he slid one finger inside her, then two, her fingers digging into the hard muscles in his upper arms.

The air grew steamy, the glass behind her slippery with condensation. She could hear the soothing sound of water through the speakers, her own ragged breathing. He wouldn't have any idea how long and often she'd dreamed about this.

Passion guided her, strengthened her, dared her to throw away inhibitions and long-held views her adoptive parents had instilled in her, and let him lead the way. To allow herself to simply feel. Oh, how liberating to follow her instincts, her wishes. To slide her hands down Steve's arms over muscle and skin and hair and feel the sinewy undulating strength in his wrists as he pleasured her. To twine her tongue with his over her teeth, over his.

To let him do whatever he wanted with her body, and give herself up to pure abandon.

Shocking.

Beautiful.

'Steve…!' The pressure built within her, every scorched nerve-ending singing, every tiny sensation stored in her mind for later. Her legs dissolved, she clung to his neck, but somehow he held her upright, the only grasp on sanity she had left. She was flying apart, shattering like that fragile glass she'd imagined earlier.

And then that final staggering release as her body tumbled

over the edge. Beyond dreams, beyond imagination, he shot her to heaven, brought her safely down.

Drained, she let her head loll against his neck, breathing in his salty skin, listening to her heartbeat slow, feeling the pulse in his throat doing double time.

Oh… 'Wow,' she breathed.

'Good,' he murmured, stroking a hand against her damp hair. 'That's good.'

As feeling returned to her legs she moved her hips and became aware of the hot ridge of arousal against her belly. She leaned back and looked down at the bulge in Steve's wet jeans. Her barely recovered pulse took another hike and a tiny shiver slid down her spine. He was…big.

But she wanted Steve. All the way. She'd always wanted Steve. And she wanted him now. Already her body ached for his touch again, the pleasure of sex he'd introduced her to was a new and exciting discovery she wanted to explore some more. But all that masculinity down there…

Following her gaze, he looked down at himself, back to her. It might have been a grin that tilted his lips, but she doubted it. More like a grimace of pain? 'Yeah,' he said, his knuckles grazing her stomach as he flicked open the stud. He tugged on the waistband, wiggled his backside. 'I think they just shrank a couple of sizes.'

She couldn't help the nervous laugh that bubbled up. 'I assume you mean the jeans?'

'The jeans.' He did grin then, but it wasn't his trade-mark casual grin, and his voice sounded more strained than cocky. 'Bit difficult to get off like this.'

'I can imagine.' She drew a shuddery breath. And wondered how they'd got to this point—making conversation about the disadvantages of denim shrinkage while stark naked and about to make love for the first time. As if this sort of thing happened every day of the week.

Maybe this *was* the way people behaved. Casual. She should try to act cool, not let him see how badly she trembled, how inexperienced she was. How *desperate* she was to have him inside her. If he knew, he might…

She heard the heavy wet plunk as his jeans and jocks hit the floor. And everything else in her mind blanked out as she took in the sight. Proud, beautiful. Fierce.

'Annie…'

She dragged her gaze to his face. Midnight eyes looked directly into hers. He cupped her cheeks and she thought she felt his arms trembling, too. Was that possible?

Then he lowered his mouth to hers, kissed her with infinite care before he murmured, 'Okay?'

She splayed her hands on the rock-solid wall of chest in front of her. 'Never better. Finish it. Now.'

All he needed to hear. Steve let out the breath he'd been holding. 'Bedroom,' he muttered, but before he could drag her into his arms and get them there her hands whipped to his shoulders, gripping him with tight ferocity, her eyes huge and dark as she looked up at him.

'Too far,' she whispered, and stepped closer. 'Now. Here.' Her hand shook as it trailed sensation over his chest, down his abdomen… He sucked in a breath as he realised where she was headed…and closed firmly around him. Exploring every hard and aching inch of him with sensual swirls and little flicks of her fingers over his tip.

Fire speared through his body; the roar in his ears sounded like a jet engine in reverse mode. Rational thought that told him to find a bed despite her protest, show her some class, deserted him.

She pressed her tight little nipples into his chest as her hand caressed him with a silky heat. Spread her legs and shifted her hips so his thigh rubbed between her slick moisture. And rode him.

And, ah, God, all he knew was tension and pressure and red-hot need. The need to lose himself in her. In Anneliese. Finally. Swamped with it, drowning in it and struggling to breathe, he had her backed up against the glass before either of them knew what happened.

She surrounded him. Her warmth, her scent, the little hitches in her breaths, her rich taste as he licked and sucked at her shoulder, her neck, her mouth.

Her urgency fuelled his own. Closing his hand over hers, he positioned himself between her legs and looked into her eyes. *Eyes that haunted his dreams.* Bright with passion now, but something flickered in their depths as she pushed down hard, impaling herself on him.

They grew even wider as she sank farther, biting her lower lip as she took him in, sheathed him inside the slick core of her body. He groaned with the pleasure. She was tight, really tight, and sweet. And hot. Rocking his pelvis, he thrust long and deep, all the way inside her once, twice, three times...

He stopped. From somewhere he found the single shred of sanity left to him and withdrew. Every muscle, even the last still-functioning brain cell screamed in protest. She'd made him forget. Everything. He clenched his jaw in frustration, self-re-crimination. *Damn.* He never forgot. Never.

'What's wrong?' she breathed as he leaned down and swiped his jeans from the floor.

'Protection.'

He heard her surprised little 'oh' as he fumbled in the pocket for his wallet—now a soggy mess—for the condom he never left home without. His fingers shook as he ripped at the foil and rolled it on.

He was blown away by the sight before him. Rubies against ivory, every curve perfection. He grasped her hands, pinned them against her head on the slippery glass, watching the way her breasts lifted, revelling in their texture as he pushed against her. Into her.

He sighed as her tight slippery passage welcomed him back. And he lost himself again as her inner muscles tightened, riding the current until he no longer knew anything but Anneliese. Until he felt the tremors shudder through her body, clenching around him. Then, and only then, with his breath labouring against her neck, his pulse pounding in his ears, he crested the final wave and came deep inside her.

Steve watched Anneliese sleep, her auburn hair turning to fire on his pillow as dawn lightened the room. Her necklace glittered at her throat. He could see the curved shadow between her breasts as she lay facing him.

He'd barely slept since he'd laid her here a few hours ago. They'd made love again during the night. Frantic, fevered, furious love, as if he couldn't get enough of her. And that connection—it was like nothing he'd ever experienced. Incredible.

He remembered the few mind-numbing moments after that first time in the elevator. He'd felt her heart beat in sync with his. With their bodies damp and still fused, he'd watched their reflections, two blurred images in the steamed-up mirrors. He'd wanted to stay there, just like that, holding Anneliese as after-shocks trembled through her. Being with Anneliese had felt…right.

Which complicated everything.

Twitching at the sheet, he turned away from the sight beside him and stared at the pumpkin-coloured sky through the floor-to-ceiling windows. Not watching her helped clear his mind, made it easier to think, to focus.

Romantic tropical setting, beautiful woman—willing woman. It was the romance, the mood; he'd told Anneliese that exact same thing only two nights ago. Because after Caitlyn there was no way on this green earth that he was going to fall all the way for a woman again. No way.

Except this was Anneliese. And…he'd never felt such a fierce protective urge towards *any* woman. And he'd done a real hatchet job on that—he'd very nearly had unprotected sex with her. There'd been a few dangerously unguarded seconds…

He shook his head. Damn. Anneliese wasn't like Caitlyn. She'd told him she wouldn't be careless enough to let herself get pregnant. Did that mean she was on the pill? Or had she simply trusted him with contraception?

Or had she never had sex before?

The thought that he might have taken her virginity cut through him like a knife. She hadn't acted as if it was her first time, but Anneliese, he was learning, was full of secrets.

With her background she might think sex implied something permanent, like marriage. She might expect more than he could give; not a good situation because he didn't intend risking the heartbreak a second time.

She snuggled closer, her thigh sliding against his, and emotion rolled through Steve. Not only did his sex stir, but a surge of something huge and deep and wide washed over him like a tidal wave as her cheek came into contact with his armpit. How would it feel to wake to her like this every morning?

No. He didn't want to think about that, because she wouldn't go for any de facto arrangement. Not Anneliese Duffield. She wouldn't settle for anything less than a fancy white church wedding and shiny band of gold on her finger.

And why was he thinking so far down the track when what he *should* be thinking about was where to from here? Today? Now?

Carefully, slowly, he removed his arm from beneath her head and lay still till she'd settled again. Then he eased out of bed and strode to the window to watch an orange sun lift out of the Pacific. The clouds had blown away and a gentle tide was rolling in.

Goose-bumps rose on his naked flesh as he stepped onto the balcony and into the cool, damp air. Anneliese was special to him, even if she'd never known it. Always had been, always would be. Which made her more than just a lover.

He rotated his shoulders and watched an early flock of gulls soar over the water. When they returned home, went back to their own routines, their own family and friends, what then?

Her father. Steve had phoned Marcus the night before they'd left Melbourne to make sure she didn't leave without him. He'd trusted Steve to take good care of his daughter, not seduce her. And Cindy… His sister wasn't going to be happy. She knew how he felt about relationships and getting involved and she would come down hard on him for messing around with her best friend.

It wasn't messing around.

And *that* fact hit him mid-chest like a tsunami crashing in from the ocean. He was falling for Anneliese. His gut tightened around the force slamming through him, his fingernails clenched into his palms. He had no idea where this would lead and right now he did *not* want to know.

Anneliese was here for some reason he still knew nothing about. He didn't want to intrude. And yet he was. He had that inevitable feeling of heading down a path that he had no control over.

CHAPTER THIRTEEN

ANNELIESE woke to the sound of Steve's voice in the other room. She couldn't hear the words, but it sounded more like business than pleasure.

Pleasure. Sliding to his side of the bed, she snuggled into his pillow, breathed in his scent. Her body had never felt so good, so complete. Because she'd just spent the night in Steve's bed. She had to say it to herself to make sure it was real. *And* she'd had the most amazing sex ever. *Well, duh,* of course it had been the most amazing sex ever.

And, oh, my stars... Her whole body flushed as she remembered. She'd had the most amazing sex because she'd climbed all over him. One orgasm—one body-zapping mind-blowing orgasm—and she'd forgotten who she was and turned into some sort of aggressive nymphomaniac.

But it wasn't only spectacular sex—it was the man himself. He was caring and considerate and fun to be with. He'd joined her in the pool, a stunt she'd never have believed she was capable of herself only a week ago. She even found herself becoming attached to his old black vest and the fact that his hair was in a permanent state of disarray and drove that dilapidated bomb of a car back in Melbourne. He didn't follow fashion or the latest sports model even though she knew he could afford it a hundred times over.

She'd spent so many years avoiding him. Not any more. With a yawn, she stretched luxuriously on the blue satin sheets. And discovered a few tight muscles she didn't know she had.

When he didn't return, she grew restless. She wanted Steve's body next to hers again. To feel him inside her, all pulsing heat and energy. She ached to re-experience that glorious place he'd sent her soaring to. Then she realised the sound she'd been only half aware of was running water and remembered they'd fallen into bed together without showering. Hmm, she should do the same.

No clothes—she guessed they were still in the elevator. She dragged the top sheet off the bed and wound it around her. Even though he'd seen every square centimetre of her body, she simply couldn't bring herself to walk through the suite without some sort of covering. Her parents had entrenched their values in her and that sort of behaviour just wasn't acceptable in her home. For the first time she found herself questioning those values.

She'd taken two steps when Steve entered the bedroom towelling his hair. Naked. His freshly shaven jaw glowed with a healthy sheen. His chest hair was freshly rubbed, looking temptingly soft and touchable. She wanted to run her hand over it again, curl the tiny hairs around her fingers. He was already semi-aroused; she tried not to notice that impressive detail as she tossed the corner of her wrap over her shoulder.

He didn't seem fazed at her perusal, in fact he seemed to take a masculine delight in it because he was growing even as she raised her eyes to his. Heat flashed in their dark depths as they met hers.

'Good morning, princess.' Throwing the towel around his neck, he crossed the carpet in three quick strides, and ran his fingers beneath her necklace along her collar-bones.

She wondered what sort of state her own hair was in and whether the remains of yesterday's make-up was evident or whether he'd kissed it all off last night.

Cool lips touched hers and lingered a moment. He smelled fresh and clean and toothpasty—unlike her. Immediately embarrassed, she stepped back, pressing her lips together. 'Umm. Hi.'

She knew he wanted her again, but he didn't try to steal her sheet. Instead he moved to the night-stand to put on his watch. A frown creased his brow. 'Annie. You'd tell me if last night was your first time. Wouldn't you?'

'Why?' Was it that obvious?

'Honesty and open communication is something I value. I'd like to think we have that. And I'd like to know. I could've made it more special for you. Last night was—'

'Wonderful. Great.' She cut him off, feeling hot and tongue-tied. She did not want to have this conversation with the playboy of the year. 'The best.' And because her cheeks were burning she turned away. 'I was just going to take a shower, too, since you—'

'It was, wasn't it?'

'Since you didn't come back to bed after your phone calls,' she finished, tightening her cotton shield.

'I didn't want to wake you. I thought you could do with some sleep. Annie…'

Then he was right behind her, turning her towards him, combing her hair off her flushed face with his fingers, gazing into her eyes with such tenderness she wanted to melt.

'You should've told me.'

'And feel inadequate?'

'No…' He shook his head, held her face between his palms and willed her to look at him. *'No.'*

Pushing at his hands, she turned away. 'I don't want to talk about it. Okay?'

'Okay...' He didn't sound happy about it. 'As long as you're all right.'

'I'm all right. Very all right. I'll just go take that shower...'

She escaped to the bathroom to press her cheeks against the cool tiles. Was he laughing at her inexperience behind her back? Yet he'd shown her understanding and concern, not the playboy she'd imagined. She unwrapped the sheet and studied her body carefully in the mirror. Then looked herself in the eye. *You have to lose your inhibitions fast if you want to keep this new relationship alive.*

Keeping that in mind, after her shower she took a quick detour to his room, then followed the aroma of coffee and bacon to the dining area, but stopped dead in her tracks. He was drinking coffee at the polished dining-room table. Fully dressed—in a *business shirt and tie*—his briefcase open on the table and a folder in front of him. So he'd decided to go to Brisbane hours after making love with her. And obviously he didn't intend making love with her again before he went. What did that tell her?

She watched him jotting notes in his folder and hugged the hotel's monogrammed terry robe against her body—her naked body—and tried not to think about the condom she'd put in its pocket on her way. Where was the Steve she'd made love with last night? The naked guy she'd seen only thirty minutes ago?

She should feel more comfortable with Steve's business persona. Here was the type of man she was accustomed to dating, the kind of man her parents introduced her to. Rich, well known, respected. Safe.

She didn't want safe and respected this morning. She wanted disreputable and dangerous. Question was, how much did she want it and was she daring enough to go get it?

As if he'd felt her watching, his gaze snapped to her. His hand froze, his pen poised in mid-air. For a beat out of time he looked stunned, as if he were seeing her for the first time, then his shoulders loosened and he smiled, his eyes still glowing with that lambent heat she'd seen last night. He put down the pen and set the folder to one side.

And suddenly those insecurities melted in that heat, and for the first time in her life Anneliese felt empowered by her femininity. Felt it course through her veins like a river of gold. Bright, beautiful, liberating. *She'd* put that glow in his eyes, that intimate smile on his lips. He'd just set aside his work for *her*.

'Hi.' He poured her a coffee, picked up his own cup. 'What do you feel like this morning?' He waved a hand, indicating the more than adequate breakfast selection he'd ordered.

'Mmm. Let's see…'

'I was going to set it on the balcony but the table's a little small for all…' He trailed off as he watched her approach.

A new woman with an appetite for more than coffee and croissants had emerged last night, and she wasn't going to lie down. Not without Steve, that was. Anneliese loosened her robe, letting the sides gape as she walked, showing him that yes, indeed, she was naked underneath, her bare feet silent on the plush carpet.

He set his cup on its saucer with a loud clink. She saw his Adam's apple bob. His eyes flickered as they slid to the deep V between her breasts. Rose to meet hers as she reached him.

'How about some of this…' Her knuckles brushed his newly shaven neck and she felt his Adam's apple bob again as she wound her hand around his tie. Easing between table and man, she spread her legs, her robe riding up to her thighs as she straddled his lap and fastened her mouth to his.

Greedy for his taste, she ran her tongue along the seam of his lips, licking inside for more when he opened to her. From where she was sitting it was obvious he liked what she was doing. She leaned back to look at him.

That same stunned gaze was back on his face. 'Annie.' His hands slid over her shoulders to curl around the edges of her robe. 'It *is* Annie, isn't it?'

'I'm not sure.' She laughed and let her head fall back, her fingers slipping from the tie to grasp his shoulders as he palmed both breasts through the cotton. She felt the contrast of warm lips and cooler air as he pressed kisses down her throat. Again that new dizzying feminine power rushed through her. 'I've never felt like this.'

He nibbled her earlobe. 'Like…how?'

'Alive. Amazing.' She kissed him again. Through the textured weave of his trousers he was hot and hard and eager to please against her bare and sensitive skin. 'So are you,' she murmured against his mouth.

'Annie…' His breath huffed out. 'I'm going to be late.' He drew the sides of her robe together, as if closing the door on temptation.

'Ooh.' It was a long-drawn-out sigh. 'Late for what?'

'An appointment.' He straightened his tie. 'And don't pout or I'll be tempted to kiss you again and we'll really be in trouble. Okay. If you sit still and promise to behave, I'll peel you a grape.'

She pouted her lips again, shrugged when he shook his head and reasoned, 'How else do you accept one measly grape?' She closed her lips around it, catching the tips of his fingers for a second before chewing.

'How about some omelette?' He spooned some up, raised it to her lips.

'No, thanks.' A sudden thought occurred to her. 'Room service delivered breakfast?'

'Yep.'

'They used the elevator.'

'Correct.'

She saw the twinkle in his eye and let out a groan. Where they'd left their clothes. And probably more body-part prints and smears on the mirrors than she wanted to think about. 'Oh. Shoot.'

He took the opportunity to slip the spoon between her lips, meeting her eyes with shared humour. She took the opportunity to wiggle closer to the heavy heat and hardness between her thighs. 'Mmm.'

He groaned and the spoon clattered to the table. 'Annie…'

'Take the day off,' she coaxed, wiggling some more. 'We can go surfing…or shopping… After.' She lifted her lips to his, letting them move in a lazy seductive motion and, in case he hadn't got the hint about *after what*, she reached down between her legs and brushed lightly at his distended fly.

'I've got a helicopter booked in thirty minutes,' he murmured against her mouth in a strangled voice.

'So unbook it. You're the boss, aren't you? Tell them an urgent matter's come up.' Bolder because she sensed his resolve waver, she moulded her fingers around him. His arousal bucked beneath her hand and she smiled against his mouth. Victory was a few sensuous strokes away—virgin to vamp overnight. 'And this urgent matter must be dealt with immediately…'

His mind a red haze of need, Steve groped for his mobile with one hand while his other hand tugged on the sash of Anneliese's robe. He yanked it open, inhaling the scent of her shower-fresh skin. 'If not sooner,' he murmured.

He circled a rosy nipple with his forefinger, watched it pucker beneath his gaze. She bit her lip and let out a stifled sound, which was some satisfaction to his own lust-crazed body. She wasn't the only one who could play tease.

He tore his eyes from the sight to glance at his phone and speed-dialled the limo service. In less than one minute he'd cancelled the ride, the chopper, his plans for the day.

When the hell had he ever been so irresponsible?

He didn't have time to remember because Anneliese loosened his tie, tugged it to one side and began undoing buttons while her hips rocked impatiently against his thighs. His phone slid from nerveless fingers and hit the carpet with a dull thud.

Which left both hands free to shrug the robe back from her shoulders. He had a second or two's glimpse of her delicate tattooed patch of skin before she dragged his attention in another direction—the snap as she undid the top button of his trousers, jerked his zipper down and freed his erection for her inspection.

And if she fingered him like that for much longer he was going to come where he sat, a waste for both of them. He dived for her hand as she arched back. 'Wait—'

The movement toppled the chair precariously. 'Wait.' Sweeping her up in his arms, robe and all, he managed the couple of metres to the Oriental blue woven silk rug in the centre of the room. He'd never wanted a woman with such urgency. His heart ticked like the sound of a timer about to detonate a bomb…any moment it would be too late if he didn't have her…now. He spread her beneath him, straddled her, then stopped, closed his eyes, teeth clenched in frustration. It was a long walk to his night-stand.

'Is this what you want?' Anneliese reached into the robe's pocket and held up a condom. 'This is the last one, so better make it worthwhile.'

He took it, smiling into those green passion-filled eyes. 'When did you get so world-wise?'

He sheathed himself in record time and pushed inside her with a groan of completion and for a moment he let the sensation wash over him. She felt like home.

Then urgency gripped him, overtook him, and as he lost

himself inside her he wondered if he'd ever find his way back to sanity again.

In the aftermath, he drew lazy circles over her stomach, and considered the fact that he'd used his entire supply of condoms. Already he wanted her again. Condoms didn't come totally without risk. And the one thing he couldn't deal with was getting Anneliese pregnant. 'Annie, we need to get you on the pill.'

Anneliese let the significance of that statement settle a few seconds before she answered. Did he ask his other lovers to take the pill? 'I'll make a doctor's appointment when we go back.'

'No.' His voice brooked no argument. 'We don't know how long we'll be here. We'll do it today.'

A few moments of silence ensued. Did it mean he intended more than a few weeks with her?

Or did it mean he wanted to make doubly sure kids were off the agenda because it was strictly a temporary thing? She wasn't sure, nor was she game to ask, especially now, with their change in relationship so new. Kids seemed to be a particularly sensitive issue with him.

He leaned over, kissed her with leisurely thoroughness, then propped himself up on one elbow and looked at her, his eyes dark and serious. 'What is it with you? Suddenly I can't be near you and not touch you. If we lie here much longer, I'll be tempted to make love with you again, and we both know that's not possible until I make a trip to the chemist. What say we take a dip in the pool and cool off?'

A slow smile touched her lips as she recalled the stunt they'd pulled. 'You think they'll let us, after last night?'

He rose and tugged on her hand. 'We'll soon find out.'

Ten minutes later Anneliese accompanied Steve downstairs, still marvelling at the ease with which she'd talked him into playing hookey. Revelling in her newly discovered femininity.

And admiring his tanned athletic legs in his shorts as they headed to the pool.

Hand in hand they strolled along the row of exclusive shops within the hotel. The scent of shampoo and nail varnish wafted from the beauty salon, the fragrance of aromatherapy products from the massage centre.

A woman exited the shop.

Anneliese's heart stopped. Except for the eyes and the hair-style, she was looking at a mirror image. She felt Steve's hand tighten reflexively on hers. Heard the other woman's startled intake of breath, or was it her own? She heard the traffic in the street, the sound of her own heart starting again only to speed up and pulse through her veins like thunder.

Her mirror image had soft grey eyes. Her hair was a riot of red curls, tied up on top of her head in a multi-hued scrunchie. She wore slim-fitting white leggings and top and smelled of sun-warmed flowers.

Abigail Seymour Forrester.

Her sister.

CHAPTER FOURTEEN

ANNELIESE took a step backwards on legs that felt like limp spaghetti. Her mouth dried to dust, her eyes pricked with pain. Who was this woman with the wide startled eyes? She didn't know her. She should feel something for her but she didn't. Not a thing. She felt nothing but an excruciating agony in her chest where her heart was, as if someone were slicing it open and letting her blood drain away on the floor.

This woman stood before her as living proof that her life had been a lie. Her family was a lie. Until now she'd hoped for some crazy reason that somehow she'd wake up and find it had all been a horrible dream. A mistake.

'I'm—'

'No!' Anneliese batted her words away, hating Abigail for shattering her dreams. Hating herself for the confusion and hurt she saw in the other woman's face—so like her own face—as she pulled out of Steve's grasp, pushed at him, then turned and ran blindly back the way she'd come.

When she reached her room, she threw herself on her bed and let the tears come. What was wrong with her? She'd come to Surfers to find her sister and when she'd finally faced her all she felt was pain. A reminder of her birth mother's rejection. The hopes she'd pinned on this meeting dashed. Because Abigail wouldn't want to know her now.

Steve stood outside Anneliese's closed door, staring at it as if it would give him an answer to his indecision. He'd been torn between following Anneliese and staying to reassure her sister—because that was obviously who she was. And now he was undecided about how long he should wait, how much time he should give her before going in and talking to her.

Answers to questions slotted into place. The reason for Anneliese's trip here. The reason why staff had looked twice at her on the couple of occasions when she hadn't been wearing her hat and sunglasses.

Abby Seymour Forrester, she'd told him, owned the hotel with her husband and would wait to hear from him or Anneliese when she was ready. That was all he knew.

The answers only raised more questions.

Like why he'd never seen or heard of a sibling. Why had Anneliese and her family kept her a secret? Annie had obviously chosen to stay at Capricorn in order to meet her, yet she'd not made contact and today's meeting had been pure chance.

The devastation he'd seen in Annie's eyes had wrapped around his heart and squeezed until he'd felt her pain as his own. His own sister flashed through his mind and the pain doubled in empathy.

He found the door unlocked, which he took to indicate she wasn't shutting him out, and allowed himself a breath of relief before tapping lightly and pushing it ajar.

He saw her facing away from him, her bikini visible through a loose sheer beach top with her bare legs drawn up to her chest. 'May I come in?'

She didn't answer, but neither did she tell him to leave. Nor did he intend to. Misery hung like an invisible shroud around her and there was no way he wasn't going to be there. 'Annie.'

He wanted to lie down beside her and take her in his arms and kiss the hurt away, but he skirted the bed and just sat beside her. 'Do you want to talk about it?'

She stared sightlessly out of swollen eyes. Still not looking at him, she held out a hand. 'I owe you an explanation.'

Encouraged—and grateful—that she was at least willing to accept his touch, he took her hand, covered it with both of his. 'You don't owe me anything, but if you want to talk, I'm listening.' In the silence that followed he heard the lazy slap of the potted palm on her bedroom balcony, the ever-present sound of the surf. 'Abigail's your sister, isn't she?' A small nod confirmed it. 'I didn't know.'

'Neither did I until a few weeks ago.' She looked up at him and the desolation he saw tore at his gut. 'I'm not Anneliese. My name's Hayley and I'm adopted. Abigail is my biological sister.'

His gut took another kick. *Adopted?* And that knowledge was obviously recent and real and painful. 'The parents who raised you and loved you made you who you are,' he said softly. He squeezed the unresponsive hand in his. 'You're Anneliese. You'll always be Anneliese to me.' *My Annie.* The revelation of those two words struck him as significant. 'When did you find out?'

'A week before we left I was clearing out Mum's clothes, trying to spare Dad the job. I found the papers in a box at the back of a drawer.' She spoke without interest, as if too drained to summon further emotion. 'I'd always assumed I was a menopause baby and Mum let me believe it. For my whole life, my parents have kept the circumstances of my birth a secret.'

'Jeez, Annie…' For the first time in their relationship he felt inadequate. 'That's a lot to cope with. How did you manage?'

'After the initial disbelief that this wasn't happening to me all I felt was numb.'

He could only try to imagine the numbness that went soul-deep. 'You didn't tell your dad.'

'No. He was dealing with Mum's death. I told no one, not even Cindy.'

Why the secrecy? 'I don't understand how you never knew. Everyone knows these days.'

'Mum and Dad are the forties generation. People back then saw it differently.'

'Surely you've had to produce a birth certificate?'

'I've never seen it. Until last week. They always did all that stuff for me—arranged my passport, my driver's licence. Everything.'

Yeah, he knew. They'd done everything for her and in so doing, they'd done her a terrible wrong.

Old pain scored the depths of his soul. The memory of Caitlyn and what she'd tried to do had sinister parallels to Anneliese's situation. Had her parents paid a king's ransom for the 'gift' of a child they knew they had no right to? He couldn't let himself get bogged down with the past. 'How did you find out about your sister?'

'I did an Internet search. She posted her details on an adoption site. She's wanted to find me her whole life.'

He could hear the sadness and the longing in her voice. Why had she run away just then? He didn't understand. 'And right now she's waiting downstairs for you, princess.'

She shook her head against the pillow, tears welling like diamonds in sad blue eyes, defeat in her voice. 'I've ruined it.'

'No.' He chafed her hand. 'Look at me. Look. At. Me.' He waited till she complied. 'It took you by surprise, that's all. She's waiting for you and she's probably just as nervous as you are. All I told her was that you're staying with me in the Pisces Suite.'

She looked at him then, her eyes widening in shock, as if

she, too, just now realised that the only person she'd trusted with this information was him.

'Sooner or later you have to face her. She's not going away—the problem's not going to go away. It's a problem only you can fix.' He gathered her up in his arms, pulling her upright and snuggling her to him. 'It's going to be okay. Trust me.' Filling his senses with her scent, so unique, so *Annie*, the sensation of her body snug against his. All the way, he thought. He was falling for Anneliese, all the way.

Anneliese curled herself against Steve's chest and closed her eyes. Her lifeline in a stormy sea. Her rock in a desert of quicksand. In revealing her story, a new awareness, a deeper trust, an added dimension to their relationship had emerged.

'I'm ready to meet my sister,' she said finally. Knowing Steve would be there for her. Knowing he cared.

Thirty minutes later she was sitting alone in another hotel room waiting. She jumped up as the door opened and Abigail stepped inside, closing the door behind her. For a moment they stared at each other.

Anneliese clutched her hands to her chest. 'Abigail.'

'Abby.' She smiled and stepped to within an arm's reach. 'Everyone calls me Abby.'

'I'm sorry about…earlier.'

'It's okay. It was a shock to me, too.'

'I'm Hayley.' The name sounded foreign on her tongue. Tentatively she reached out to touch smooth skin. Warm flesh. Family. 'My name's Anneliese now and I came here to find you.'

Abby took that final step to wrap her arms around her sister and a thousand emotions ran through Anneliese but none was more overwhelming than love and relief.

'You know,' Abby whispered against her ear, 'when I was very good, our mother used to let me feed you your bottle.'

'Our mother.' The words wrenched her in two. Torn between the mother she'd known and lost, and an unknown woman who'd given her life. 'You knew her.'

Abby's cheek rubbed against hers. 'She died, honey. She loved us—she'd never have left us by choice. And I was too young to do anything about it when they took you away from me.'

Finally Anneliese drew away, sniffing. 'Tissues.'

'I know.' Abby sniffed, too, and smiled through her tears. 'Never a tissue handy when you need one. Lucky I came prepared.' She pulled a purse pack from the embroidered pouch at her waist. 'You're coming home with me tonight. We have a lifetime of catching up to do.'

'Ah…Steve…'

'Is invited, too, of course.'

'That was a fantastic meal,' Steve told their hostess as they lingered over their drinks in Abby and Zak's open-space living room. The aroma of barbecued prawns and steak still wafted from the outdoor grill on the veranda. Abby's foster-mum, Aurora, a delightful eccentric, had excused herself and retired for the evening.

'You're very welcome,' she told him. 'We both love cooking.'

The couple shared an intimate smile before Annie said, 'Tell me about the wedding.'

'It was just our vows, a pretty dress and a seafood smorgasbord with Aurora's and Zak's family and friends. We didn't care how we were married, so long as we were.'

'How long did you know Zak before you knew it was the real thing?' she asked.

'Do you believe in love at first sight? It was kinda like that.' Abby's eyes glazed over. 'It just took a little longer to convince

Zak.' She laughed, a tinkling sound that echoed her jewellery. 'He was damn hard work, I can tell you.'

Over a stunning glass of shiraz, Steve watched the titian-haired sisters talk and pondered how life's experiences carved one's personality. They were like the opposing sides of a bright copper coin. Alike yet different. Abby had been brought up in foster homes, Anneliese had enjoyed the best wealth and privilege could buy.

Abby was a whirlwind of blues, baubles and bare feet, Anneliese, serenity in a cream off-the-shoulder dress and matching camisole with spiky silver shoes. Where Abby's hair was a riot of curls, Anneliese's bob didn't have a hair out of place.

He'd always gone for the outgoing, fun-loving type like Abby. Until Anneliese. At that moment she looked over and met his eyes and her serenity ruffled a little around the edges as electricity arced between them, jolting his heart into an uneven rhythm.

Then Abby excused herself to go to the bathroom and Anneliese rose and walked into the kitchen. Steve heard the sound of a sliding door and knew she'd gone outside to the veranda.

'If I was you, I'd follow,' Zak said a moment later.

Unsure, Steve ran his thumbs over his glass. 'Maybe it's better if Abby does.'

'You know her better than I do,' Abby said, overhearing him as she re-entered the room. Her hands rubbed over Steve's shoulders. 'Go.'

When he reached the door he saw her leaning against the railing, talking on her mobile phone. He was about to backtrack when she disconnected. He stepped into the evening air. 'Everything okay?'

Her lips curved into a smile as she slipped her phone into

her purse. 'Everything's fine. I was talking to Dad. Cindy's there. They're eating tea together.' She looked directly into his eyes. 'You organised Cindy to watch out for him, didn't you?'

He slipped his hands into the back pockets of his jeans. 'Friends help each other out.'

That was what they'd been when he'd arranged it with Cindy: friends. But they'd been more than friends for a few days now. Perhaps even more than lovers. And that notion still sat uneasily with Steve.

She stood just outside the spill of light from the kitchen, but it was enough for him to see the emerald in her eyes darken. 'Thank you.' She looked out over the lush garden. 'I can't tell him about this over the phone but I want to stay on a bit.'

The low and lazy sound of wood and bamboo wind-chimes moving slowly in the breeze filled the air. He came up behind her, rested his chin on the top of her head. 'Then we'll stay on a bit.'

Steve got his wish as he lay down beside her that night—moon-light streamed across the bed, its cool light painting Anneliese's body silver, giving her that ethereal glow that suited her personality so well.

Yet he'd seen another side, a passionate Anneliese that fired his blood as no one ever had. But not tonight. Tonight she needed slow and tender. Understanding. She didn't need words and neither did he. He lifted her arm and kissed his way along the tender inner skin, the inside of her wrist, her palm.

Her eyes glittered in the half-light, dark with desire as he explored her body with a languid hand. He took his time to love every inch of her body. With his hands. With his mouth. Her neck, collar-bone, behind her ear. He gave equal attention to each plump breast, her nipples cherry-dark in the moon-glow, enjoying the way she arched against him.

Every part of her body had its own flavour, its own texture, every curve and dip its own fragrance. *Body, mind and spirit.* He pressed a kiss to each symbol in turn before tracing his hands down her thighs, her calves. Every toe.

And when he couldn't wait any longer, he slid inside her with a sigh that seemed to wrap like a quiet peace around them both.

He understood her. Her pain. Her strengths. Her weaknesses. And she was like no other woman he'd ever known.

The next week passed in a whirl of discovery for Anneliese. Learning about Abby and her mum and a life Anneliese didn't remember but saw through her sister's eyes. Shopping with Abby for Steve…and herself, lunching with Steve in Brisbane when he sent the helicopter for her. Sharing her thoughts and hopes on her new-found family with Steve. And lying in his arms every night.

She loved him. She'd loved him for ever and the knowledge was a treasure she guarded in her heart.

He never mentioned returning to Melbourne or what might happen to their relationship when they went home, but with every passing day she wondered. It kept her awake in the wee small hours. Sometimes when she woke, he was awake, too. She wanted to ask him what kept him from sleep, but the words wouldn't come. At those times, they turned to each other and made slow, deep love.

But something else had kept her awake for the past couple of nights. She was overdue. She was never overdue. Her cycle was as regular as the clock ticking the minutes till she could breathe easy and start her contraceptive pills.

She put it down to the recent upheaval in her life.

He obviously didn't see a future and family with her, and

she kept hidden the wounded corner of her soul that longed for what she couldn't have. He'd never made promises he didn't intend to keep.

'When we go back I think we should date for a while,' Steve said over breakfast.

His work in Brisbane was almost done and they planned on flying home in a couple of days. Her car had already been transported home by rail.

At last he'd brought the topic they hadn't discussed into the open, she thought, and said, 'As in you ask me out and drop me off at the front door at the end of the night?'

He reached over the table to slide his knuckles up and down her nape. No doubt his years of dating experience put the glint in his eye as he said, 'A lot can happen before we get to your front door, Annie.' He took a last sip of coffee. 'It'll be fun. Give us a chance to see how we fit in the real world. Surprise Cindy. Most importantly, it'd be nice for your dad.' He paused. 'You haven't told them, have you?'

'No.' Because Anneliese hadn't been sure how it would be between them back home. 'What if I don't want to please my dad?'

'Well, I do. He trusted me to look after you, not sleep with you. You're feeling angry, but that's normal, and temporary.'

She nodded half-heartedly. For once her mind wasn't on the conversation. 'I guess.' She drummed nervous fingers on her thigh. For the first time she wished Steve would hurry up and go. Too bad he'd chosen this morning to start relationship negotiations.

'You're edgy this morning, princess.' He patted his mouth on the cloth napkin and rose, then sat down again, his brows drawing together as he covered her hand with his. 'You do want to explore this relationship further, don't you?'

She turned her hand palm up and entwined her fingers with his. 'Yes.' But how would he feel if circumstances changed? 'Of course I do.'

'Then what is it?'

'Nothing.' She summoned a smile. 'Abby and I are going shopping in a while and I'm not nearly ready.' She glanced down at her robe, the only stitch of clothing she wore at the moment.

'Okay, I can take a hint.' He squeezed her hand then kissed her lips.

She wondered if that would be the last time he ever kissed her and found herself clinging to his neck a fraction longer than usual.

He frowned again, his eyes darkening as he leaned back and searched her face. 'Are you sure there's nothing wrong?'

'Yes.' She smiled and made a shooing motion with her hands. 'Go.'

Anneliese sat at the dining room table staring at the box she'd purchased moments ago downstairs. She couldn't be pregnant. She just couldn't be. *Go on*, the little voice whispered again. *Prove it.*

Five minutes later, she had her proof.

She stared at the double line on the test stick. The world as she knew it disappeared for ever. And she'd thought her life complicated before.

CHAPTER FIFTEEN

As IF by magic, the knowledge that she was pregnant was a trigger for a wave of nausea. Anneliese collapsed onto the edge of the spa, rinsed a face towel with cold water and pressed it to her neck. She loved a man who didn't want children and she was having his baby.

Her hand dropped to her belly without conscious thought. She remembered his decisive words: *Family life's not for me.* And the twisted pain she'd seen behind his eyes when he'd said it. If only he'd opened up, she might understand, but he'd been tight as a clam—

Abby's knock on the door dragged her up out of the lonely and scary place she suddenly found herself in. She hurried to the door and let her in.

'Ready?' Abby said, breezing in with a soft tinkle of jewellery.

'I'll just…run a comb through my hair…'

She backed away and hurried to the bedroom, hearing Abby call, 'It looks perfect to me,' as Anneliese checked her face in the mirror. Did she look different or was it her imagination?

She turned away. She didn't have time for soul-searching. Grabbing her bag from the bed, she hurried to the door but her steps slowed. She couldn't go shopping today. She had to figure out what she was going to do. Somehow she had to put Abby off.

But when she re-entered the room Abby was holding the empty box Anneliese had left on the table. Abby studied her a moment. 'Good news?'

Anneliese pulled out a chair and sat. 'I'm pregnant.'

'The question still stands, Annie.'

'Steve doesn't want kids.' The pain sliced through her anew.

Abby reached out a hand. 'Oh, honey. Sure he does, with the right woman. And you're that woman—I can tell just by looking at the two of you.'

Anneliese shook her head. 'No.'

'Okay, how do *you* feel about it?'

Abby's words forced Anneliese to confront her new-found knowledge. 'I want this baby,' she realised. Nothing and nobody was going to change that.

'You need to tell Steve. Let him decide what he wants to do.'

The thought made her tremble inside and out. According to her rough calculation, when he'd insisted she take the pill it had already been too late. But he didn't know that. He'd see this as some sort of betrayal. 'I can't tell him while he's at work. I'll have to wait until tonight.'

Abby squeezed her hand. 'That'll give you time to—'

Anneliese's mobile chimed, interrupting Abby and shredding Anneliese's already jaded nerves. The unfamiliar disembodied voice from a Melbourne hospital told her that her father had been taken to Emergency with severe pain. They didn't know the cause yet, but would keep her informed.

'Dad's been rushed to hospital,' she said. Guilt pounded through her veins as she pushed up. The last image of him standing on the veranda waving goodbye flashed before her eyes. She deliberately hadn't told him she loved him before she left. And, no matter what had happened, *he* was the one man who loved her unconditionally. She'd never, ever forgive herself if he— 'I have to get home. I have to ring Steve, book a flight, pack—'

'You ring Steve and pack only what you need for now. I'll book the flight.' Abby spoke calmly, her voice soothing in the face of panic.

Anneliese nodded and speed-dialled Steve. He'd left his phone on voice message so she outlined the situation and hurried to pack a few essentials.

Abby drove her to the airport. 'I'm sorry it ended this way,' Anneliese said through a haze of tears. 'Just when we were getting to know each other.'

'It's not for long, little sister. Concentrate on your dad for now, and that little bundle of joy in there.' She patted Anneliese's belly, then kissed her cheek. 'I'll fly down in a few weeks and spend some time. Prayers for your dad.'

Late in the evening, Anneliese took a cab from Tullamarine Airport straight to the hospital. She'd phoned as soon as they touched down and was relieved to hear he wasn't in danger. *Thank you, God.*

In fact when she arrived at his room he was chirpy enough to be joking with the nursing staff. His face lit up like Cavill Avenue on a Saturday night when he saw her. She stood a moment, drinking in the sight. He was her father in every way that counted. She rushed to his bed and flung herself at him with a tearful, 'Daddy.'

'Hello, bunnykins.'

'I love you.' How good it was to be able to say it. Finally she dragged herself up to search his face. *'Food poisoning?'*

He grinned. 'You know me, Annie, can't boil an egg to save myself. I'm fine now, but a little tired.'

The guilt still plagued her. If she'd been here this might not have happened. 'You've been working too hard. It's time to retire and enjoy your life now.'

'I'm seriously thinking about it. In fact when they let me out of here tomorrow I'm spending a week in that luxury new rehab centre near home.'

'Sounds like a great idea.' She paused. 'Daddy—'

'Anneliese, I—'

Both spoke at the same time.

She nodded. 'You first.'

'You found your adoption papers amongst your mother's private documents, didn't you?'

'Yes.' Guilt heated her cheeks. 'I wasn't snooping.' Oh, but partial relief flooded through her—news she didn't have to break. 'I was sorting.'

'I know.' He suddenly looked tired, old, sad. 'You don't know how sorry I am that you had to find out that way. We should have told you years ago.'

'Ah, Dad,' she sighed. 'Why didn't you?'

'We thought we'd lose you, and the longer we put it off, the worse it got.' He shook his head. 'And you know how your mother was—her whole life, her world, was centred around you.'

She remembered countless times she'd had to come back from school camps and, as she grew older, interstate trips, because her mother had taken ill, only to miraculously recover on her return. Her mother had loved her, perhaps too much. Anneliese wouldn't have hurt her for the world. She closed a hand over his. 'You'd never have lost me, Dad. I love you. But I had another family out there I never knew about. A sister.'

He linked his fingers through hers. 'I'd like to meet her some time.'

'You will. She's coming to Melbourne when you're well enough. It's okay, Dad. Everything's going to be okay.'

But when she rang Steve later from home to update him on her father, she wondered how true those words would be. Steve was coming home as planned, in two days. Two days to think about how she was going to tell him her news.

'I've got my own news to announce,' Cindy said, filling two champagne glasses. Anneliese had told her about her adoption and Abby in a two-hour phone call a few nights ago from Surfers. They were sitting cross-legged on the ageing sofa in her living room, sharing a tub of cherry ice cream Cindy had pulled from the freezer and half a bottle of champagne and listening to a loud Robbie Williams singing about entertaining them. 'I finally got that promotion I was after.'

'So that's the reason for the celebration.' Anneliese raised her glass. 'Congratulations.'

'And I've decided to move out to be nearer work. Still, anything's enough reason to break out the bubbly, don't you agree?'

'Actually, I've been trying to stay off the stuff,' she began, trying not to alert Cindy to the fact that she wasn't touching alcohol. 'I had a bad experience in Surfers.'

'Oh?'

'It's okay now. I'd just prefer apple juice, if you have it.'

'Coming right up.' When they were settled again Cindy said, 'So, how did you and Steve get along?'

Anneliese's breath hitched. 'Fine.' She took a sip of juice, gritted her teeth and decided now was as good a time as any to say, 'Speaking of Steve, what is it with him? Has he got something against kids?'

'Caitlyn.' Cindy's mouth twisted, her spoon halfway to her mouth. 'The wickedest witch who ever walked this earth.' Cindy's face contorted with an anger Anneliese had never seen before.

'What happened?'

Cindy drew a breath. 'He met Caitlyn nine years ago at the tender age of twenty-three and fell fast and hard. According to Steve, they were going to get married.'

Anneliese's heart beat faster, just thinking about how it would feel to have him say they were getting married.

'He was just getting Angel-Shield Security off the ground and putting all the money he had into the business,' Cindy continued. 'Then Caitlyn got pregnant. And that's when Steve learned she was using him—as a sperm donor.'

Anneliese sucked in a disbelieving breath. 'Oh, my God.'

'She planned to sell their baby to a wealthy couple who couldn't have kids.'

A wealthy couple who couldn't have kids… Like Anneliese's parents. The whole panorama rolled through her mind, making her head spin, and she had to brace her hands on the table for support. 'That doesn't make sense. If she planned the pregnancy for something like that, why would she tell him about it? Why not have a one-night stand?'

'My guess would be she wanted regular, safe sex until she conceived.' She shook her head, setting her pony-tail swinging. 'And, *oh, no*, she did not tell him about the baby. That was a secret she kept all to herself.

'It doesn't matter how at this point in time, but Steve found out the whole sordid story. Naturally, being the nurturing kind of guy he is, it devastated him. He offered her half share in his business in exchange for the baby, but she laughed and told him his business would never make the kind of money this couple could offer her. The irony is in these past years he's made that money ten times over.

'When he threatened to sue for custody of his unborn child she terminated the pregnancy, moved interstate and probably went on to destroy someone else's life, and we never saw her again. Thank God.'

'That's...just *horrible*.' Anneliese steepled her hands and covered her nose and mouth. Her whole body felt as if it had been knocked sideways.

Cindy blew out a breath. 'Which is why Steve has major problems with attachments. I'm the only person in his life who's stayed.'

This time, Anneliese thought, it wouldn't be the woman who walked. It would be Steve.

'Enough about Steve. I'm going clubbing with the girls from work in an hour,' she said. 'I know it's not your usual scene, but why don't you come with us? It's Friday night—the city will be buzzing.'

'Not tonight. I'm tired after everything that's happened with Dad and Abby.'

'Sure.' Cindy nodded sympathetically.

The sound of the front door opening jump-started Anneliese's heart into action. The stereo masked any sound of approaching vehicles, leaving Anneliese unprepared for seeing Steve. Before she could brace herself, there he was.

The familiar punch she always felt when she caught that first glimpse of him curled into a knot beneath her ribs.

In a charcoal-grey well-cut suit and maroon tie, he looked swoon-worthy. His snowy shirt was travel-creased but still gorgeous against his olive skin. His brown eyes met hers and held briefly.

It must have taken less time than an indrawn breath, but a dozen different emotions skidded through Anneliese. Energy arced across the room between them, leaving residual heat shimmering on her skin. Even a few steps away, his woodsy aftershave permeated her senses. Her fingers tingled with the need to touch. To creep beneath that suit jacket, undo the buttons on his shirt and absorb the warmth of all that skin, and then—

His gaze flicked between them. 'Hi, you two.'

'Hi.' Cindy uncurled herself from the sofa. 'We didn't expect you back till tomorrow.'

'I managed to get away early.' His glance at Anneliese as Cindy met him in the middle of the room for her customary kiss said, *To see you, Annie*.

But the 'dating' thing was still on as far as Anneliese knew. They hadn't discussed it since he'd first mentioned it yesterday morning. Their phone calls had been filled with Dad's recovery—hurried calls because Steve had been busy finishing his work.

Suddenly this changed relationship with Steve, the exchange of different kinds of glances and a whole new set of rules, confused her. It took all her restraint to watch him kiss his sister on the cheek and know she wasn't going to get one. To paste on a smile and say, 'Hello, Steve,' the way she always did.

'Hi, Anneliese. How's your dad doing?'

'He's going to be fine.'

'That's good to hear.'

Steve grinned at Anneliese over his sister's head. He hadn't expected to see her here. He'd planned on driving over the moment he arrived home and he hadn't phoned her because he'd wanted to surprise her by turning up a day earlier. She was wearing skinny jeans and a hot red top, a new look for her. Damn, but he wanted to walk right over and kiss her senseless. Why the hell had he suggested dating?

'We've been late-night shopping.' Cindy collected the remains of their snack and carried it to the kitchen. 'We detoured here for sustenance. I'm dropping Annie home in a moment.'

Perfect. He saw the flash in her eyes and just knew what she was thinking and his skin crawled with heat. 'I'll take you home,' he said. How many sleepless hours last night had he lain awake missing her?

Thinking about her.

Thinking how he felt about her.

Thinking what to do about her.

He positioned himself so he had his back to his sister and gave Annie a conspiratorial grin. 'We travelled seventeen hundred k's together, Annie. I reckon we can manage ten without too many problems.'

He turned back to see Cindy nod across the servery that divided kitchen and living room. 'Would you mind, Annie? It'll give me time for a quick shower before I meet the girls. I was going to go as I am, but…'

'Of course.' Anneliese picked up a plastic store-carry bag, shrugged into a fluffy white jacket and went around the servery to hug Cindy. 'Have a good night. Talk to you soon.'

Cindy turned to her brother. 'I won't be home tonight—I'm sleeping over at Lisa's.'

'Okay.' Without thinking, his eyes flicked to Anneliese's for a millisecond, then away. 'Ring me if there's a change in plans.'

Anneliese was waiting at the front door before he'd pulled his keys out of his trouser pocket. Her perfume… He breathed in that familiar scent as she walked ahead of him across the veranda and down the front steps. The slow burn of anticipation flickered along his veins.

The moment they rounded the corner of the house he wrapped his hand around one fluffy arm and spun her to face him. 'Annie.' He absorbed the shape of fine bone and muscle through the fabric, felt her soft rapid exhalations of breath against his face, and the slow burn flared into life.

'You're back early.' Her voice was sandpaper rough, equal parts accusation and desire.

'Are you complaining?' Both hands now, because one wasn't enough, he gripped her upper arms, pressed her against the wall and laid his lips on hers.

Texture. Taste. Her tongue colliding with his. The low keening sound in her throat. He tilted his pelvis as she rolled her hips against the wall, against him. His hands dived beneath her jacket to find her breasts. Her quick breaths puffed out into the chill air.

He looked into her eyes, eyes that burned with desire yet hinted at vulnerability. He'd seen that same look on their last morning in Surfers. 'Come on.' He heard the gruffness in his tone as he grabbed her hand and tugged her to the four-bay garage at the back of the house. He flicked a remote and one of the two double-roller doors rumbled up, revealing his tired ute with its faded bodywork.

He unlocked the passenger door. The engine sputtered its displeasure when he turned the ignition over several times. 'Hasn't been used in a few weeks,' he murmured.

'Please tell me why you keep this car when you could have any car you want.'

'Because this *is* the one I want.' While the engine sputtered to life and warmed up he switched on the interior light and ran a loving hand over the dash.

'It's only a two-seater.'

'Great for me and my line of work. Toss everything in the tray at the back. I can still take Cindy wherever she wants to go if she needs a lift.'

'And if I wanted to come, too?'

He grinned. 'We'd just have to squeeze up a little.'

'Illegal. No seat belt.'

'Okay, we throw you over the back with the security equipment. Don't worry, if I need the extra space there's always Dad's Audi.' He pointed to the shadowy end of the garage and an immaculate-looking silver car. 'I don't use it very often.' He turned his attention to reversing.

'This dating thing's ridiculous,' she said as he turned his attention to reversing. 'Aren't we a little old to be sneaking around?'

'It could be fun.' For a couple of days.

A minute later he turned off the main road and pulled over to the kerb in a tree-lined side-street. Her eyes glittered in the dashboard lights; her lips looked hot and luscious and inviting. Like the rest of her. 'Cindy's going out. Come back home with me.'

'There's no one at my place.'

'Ah, but you have reverse cycle air-con, we have an open fireplace and I still have this fantasy of you and firelight.'

Her eyes flashed hot, then wary. 'I don't have…'

'A nightgown?' *I promise you, you won't need one.*

A slightly nervous laugh bubbled up. 'A toothbrush?' Steve smoothed her hair behind her ear. 'I have a spare. We can go for a drive to the city first, make sure Cindy's gone.' *If I can wait that long.*

Anneliese bit her lip but a smile spilled over. 'This time I won't be sleeping over with Cindy.'

Steve pressed his mouth to that smile in a brief, hard kiss. 'You won't be getting much sleep with me either,' he promised.

CHAPTER SIXTEEN

ANNELIESE WATCHED THE long length of his spine as Steve set a match to the kindling in the living-room fireplace. He'd removed his suit jacket and tie, rolled up his sleeves.

She rubbed her arms in the chill of the room and the chill that wrapped cold fingers around her heart. One more time with him. One more night in his arms before he walked away. 'What if Cindy comes home?'

Dusting off his hands, he turned to her. 'She's not coming home. Relax. We've got all night.' His lips moved over hers in a slow kiss—meant to calm? Or arouse.

He switched off the overhead light, leaving the room bathed in flickering red. His shirt glowed crimson as the flames caught and rose. He peeled off her fluffy jacket, put it on the couch. 'Music?'

She looked into the fire, then into his eyes. 'Your choice.'

'I've got the perfect CD—romantic piano. Wine or…?'

'Tia Maria. Please.'

Liqueur should be her last choice. But Tia Maria was her favourite, why not have it tonight? This last night with Steve. Except she was pregnant, so she only intended to moisten her mouth with it. She sat down on the couch while Steve put on the music and listened to a melody from a romantic movie while he disappeared to the kitchen for glasses.

He returned with two crystal glasses of rich dark liquid, set them on the hearth before pulling a soft-looking throw-rug from the carved camphor wood box that doubled as their coffee-table. He spread it on the floor, then knelt before the fire, picked up the glasses, held one out to her. 'Come here, Annie.'

Taking the tiny glass from his fingers, Anneliese knelt in front of him as a Latin number drifted from the speakers, its lazy beat throbbing in the air. Gazes locked, they raised their drinks. Together they inhaled the rich chocolate-coffee bouquet. Let its velvet texture flow over their tongues as they sipped.

It was a moment of sensual intimacy that stunned and seduced. One to remember. Then he licked the sticky liquid from her lips, kissed her once. Slowly, deeply.

And somehow the glasses were gone and Steve's hands stroked down her hair, her face, her neck in one slow, smooth movement. Over the swell of her breasts, so lightly she felt it more intensely—if that were possible—every fingertip, every fingernail a trail of pleasure. And all the while his eyes remained on hers, hot and dark and potent.

He didn't yet know her news.

Without breaking eye contact, she crossed her arms to pull the hem of her top up and over her head. Her nipples puckered beneath her new red bra and she saw that his gaze had dropped to her breasts. All her blood seemed to rush there, making them feel full and heavy. She watched his nostrils flare, his chest expand as he sucked in a breath.

She sucked in her own breath, caught her bottom lip with her teeth as she unclasped her bra, slid the straps down her arms and discarded it beside her. 'Your turn,' she said. 'Take off your shirt.'

'You're doing such a magnificent job…' His voice was low, thick, husky.

She didn't know if he meant for her to continue her strip-tease or to help him. Her choice, then, so she leaned forward, her fingers trembling a little as she slipped the top button of his shirt free, then the next, her knuckles grazing hot flesh as she worked her way down over hard muscle and hairy skin.

And it was a spectacular sight as she pushed the fine fabric over his broad shoulders gleaming bronze in the firelight. A wonderful feeling as her fingers slid between shirt sleeves and the ropey sinews in his arms as she pushed the fabric to his wrists.

She couldn't help herself; she leaned forward to rub her lips over the patch of skin she knew so well—the hollow below his Adam's apple. To breathe in the scent of musky man. Of Steve.

Her breath caught as his palms slid beneath her breasts, cupping them and taking their weight. Then he rose, and catching her hands in his, he pulled her up. Slowly. So her body grazed the rock-hard length of his erection, the smooth metal belt buckle and finally firm muscle beneath warm, naked skin.

They didn't need words; they moved in sync. As if watching a mirror, they toed off shoes, tugged off socks. Anneliese unzipped her jeans and stepped out of them while he pulled a foil packet from his pocket and tossed it down between them.

Her gaze fell to the floor, then flicked to his. *If only you know.* Heat rushed up her neck as he unzipped his trousers and let them fall where he stood. Pushed them out of the way. Jocks and panties were shimmied out of and kicked aside.

'Ah…Annie. You're beautiful in firelight. I can hardly bear to touch you, you're so perfect.'

His words, the emotion in his raw-throated voice, spun through her like diamonds. 'Don't let me down,' she said softly. 'I'm counting on you touching me.' Very slowly. Very thoroughly. All over.

The fire's glow streaked his skin bronze and black and gold.

Awed, she took in every centimetre of his masculine beauty. The honed athletic body, the primal aroused male. Stripped bare, no secrets.

No secrets.

He reached out a hand to her; she met it palm to palm. They sank to the rug together, and Steve stretched out beside her, facing her. His eyes turned to molten chocolate and she felt the tremor in his hand as he stroked her from neck to navel, reached down to the soles of her feet. And every place in between; one feather-light pass with those long blunt fingers.

He lay back and watched her as she repeated the action over his body.

He reached over, dipped his finger in her glass. Then drew a sticky circle around her navel. Heat chased cool as he blew on her belly, then licked the liqueur away. Her fingers fisted in his hair and her breathing grew ragged, but he didn't stop there. He repeated the procedure lovingly on both breasts, until she could barely lie still.

She tightened her hold on his hair. 'Enough with the slow.' She knew she sounded desperate. At this point she didn't care.

He lifted his head to look at her, a devilish glint in his dark eyes. 'I love it when Anneliese Duffield loses that cool control.' He kissed the space between her breasts, shifted upwards to drop kisses on her neck, her jaw, her lips. 'I love that I can make you lose it.'

He reached for the condom packet, ripped it open and rolled the protection on. He moved on top of her then and she welcomed his warmth and weight with a moan of pleasure. Another moan as the tip of his erection nudged between her legs. As he slid into her like a hot knife through butter. They both groaned as she tilted her hips, as her muscles clamped around him, drawing him in.

'You still want to go slow?' she breathed against his ear and drew her inner muscles up tighter.

He jerked inside her. 'Yes-s-s.' And sucked in a breath. 'Where *did* you learn to do that?'

She just smiled. 'Now who's losing control?' She did it again, loving the still-new sensation of all that pulsing hardness inside her. Knowing it would be the last time.

'Never.' He pulled out slowly, slowly, deliberately sliding his length over a particularly sensitive spot until he was barely inside. His arms were braced either side of her, taking his weight, and they weren't steady. Neither was his breathing.

She glared at him. His eyes were hot and hungry but devilishly amused as she writhed upwards in an effort to get nearer. 'Not fair,' she managed, between her struggles. Then gave up and fell back limp. Futile to think she could match him at this game.

He touched his brow to hers. 'All's fair, princess.' And began the exquisitely slow return journey.

So she clamped her teeth over her lip and let him go slow. She endured the endless glorious torture he lavished on her and told him she loved him with her eyes.

Tomorrow morning everything would change.

Steve watched daylight slip into his room, turning the whole room to gold. Anneliese. His chest tightened. He'd spent the night with her in this room. He turned to find her side of the bed empty, then heard the sound of a tap running in the bathroom and relaxed back again.

No woman had ever made it past his bedroom door. Until now. He slept alone here. Had done for the past eight years. Cindy shared the house; she didn't need to meet his lovers. They weren't in his life for more than a few weeks, a couple of months; not long enough to get to know, leastways not the way Cindy would know them.

But she knew this one.

And this one was special.

She made him remember things he'd blocked from his mind and from his heart. Things he'd never wanted to feel again, not after Caitlyn.

Too late.

Because Anneliese was the woman he loved.

His fingers tightened at his sides. He was fair dinkum, big time, all the way in love with Anneliese Duffield.

He loved her innocent *naïveté* and the joyful exuberance of discovery as a whole new world opened up to her. Her loyalty to her parents even to the detriment of her own happiness. To Cindy and Abby. To him.

Hints of the spoilt princess still lurked and a half-smile curved his lips momentarily. Hard to change a lifetime of behaviour. And he wouldn't change a thing. Not a thing. That was Anneliese and he loved her just the way she was.

He wished she'd hurry back to bed so they could make love again.

But all his insecurities, his fear of making attachments, flooded back. His reasons for not getting involved; live for today, forget tomorrow. Caitlyn had ruined his perception of what marriage and family and commitment could be. Anneliese didn't deserve to be the recipient of those perceptions. In his heart he knew she'd never deceive him.

Could he risk commitment again? He'd taken a big step towards making that commitment last week with something he hoped Anneliese would like. A surprise he'd keep for a couple more weeks. And he had a few ideas for the dating game they were going to play first.

Anneliese regarded herself in the mirror. She'd barely slept, counting down the hours, the last minutes till he wanted nothing more to do with her. She'd risen early, picked up her clothes strewn over the living-room floor and dressed. She'd called a cab to take her home. It was waiting on the kerb outside the house.

With a last look in the mirror, she took a breath and entered the bedroom.

He opened his eyes as she stepped to the bed. 'Hi.' His sleepy smile dimmed. 'What's with the clothes?'

She bent down for one last, lingering kiss. One kiss to last the rest of her life. Then she straightened. 'Can you come to the living room? I have something I need to tell you and I'd rather tell you there.'

He stared at her a moment and she saw his jaw tighten. 'Why do I get the feeling it's not something I want to hear?'

She didn't answer, but walked down the passage and stood by the fireplace. The smell of cold ash permeated the room. How appropriate, she thought.

He appeared in the doorway in nothing but track-pants. She wished he'd put on a T-shirt, at least, so she wouldn't have to look at all that bronzed male nakedness.

'Okay. What do you want to say?'

She sucked in a breath and forced herself to meet his eyes. 'I'm pregnant.' And just in case he didn't get it the first time— 'I'm having a baby. Your baby.'

Silence.

She watched, desperate for some sign, but it was as if he'd turned to stone, except for his Adam's apple, which bobbed once. His complexion had turned to a whiter shade of pale. And his wide-eyed gaze dipped to her waist.

'How long have you known?' His lips flattened and his voice sounded as if he'd dragged it over hot coals.

'A couple of days.'

His head fell back and he gazed at the ceiling a moment, then returned that dark tortured gaze to hers. 'What the hell happened to the pill you were supposed to be taking?'

'It happened before I started them.' She saw disbelief flicker in his eyes. 'It was already too late. Believe it or not, as you like.'

'Who else have you told?'

'No one. I wouldn't tell anyone until you knew, Steve.' If it was possible, that dark gaze turned darker. 'It's okay. I can do this on my own if I have to. I'm sorry.'

'Why are you apologising? We were both there.'

Yes. And they'd have an everlasting reminder of that time in Surfers Paradise. 'I know this is the last thing you want.'

His blade-sharp eyes reached deep inside her, leaving nothing unscathed. 'Is this the last thing *you* want?' he said slowly.

She saw his emotion, held in check by rigid self-control. The tight fists and clenched jaw. And impossible to miss the wonder—and the fear—in his gaze.

Her hand moved to her stomach. 'I want this baby. This baby will be loved. Is already loved. And *no one* will ever take this baby away from me.'

Steve dropped his gaze to her protective hand. Every muscle was under lock-down. Every beat of his heart drummed in his ears. He wanted to reach out and touch her, to touch the place where his baby lay, but he couldn't move. 'Pregnant,' he murmured, his mind spinning with dreams he'd slammed the door on long ago. 'Sweet heaven.'

'Who's pregnant?' Cindy strolled in chomping on an apple, then stopped, staring at the remains of last night—Steve's clothes strewn on the floor, a bottle of liqueur and two used glasses.

'You're back early.' He was surprised he could raise his voice above a croak when everything inside him was tangled in knots. Neither of them had heard her arrive.

'I'm looking at apartments today. Just in case you forgot,

I'm moving out…' Her questioning gaze switched to Anneliese. 'Sorry I wasn't here. Did we arrange to go somewhere this morning?'

'No.' Steve watched Anneliese meet his sister's eyes. 'And it's me who's pregnant.'

'Oh…*Annie*.' She crossed the room and took Anneliese by the shoulders. 'Why didn't you tell me last night? I could've… Who…?' Her gaze took in the scene, then suspicious brown eyes met Steve's.

His heart squeezed in his chest as he remembered Anneliese's eyes, the way she'd looked at him, and he at her as they'd made love by the fire. He'd felt as if he were falling endlessly—

'What the *hell* is going on here?' Cindy's demand cut through his lost dreams.

'Annie and I—'

The fist she planted squarely in his chest reverberated through his bones and had him stumbling back a step. 'How *could* you? My best friend, my *innocent* best friend. And my brother.' The last she uttered on a sigh as she closed her eyes and he knew she was trying not to imagine the two of them together.

His own cheeks rioted with heat. 'It's none of your business, Cindy. We're two consenting adults. We don't need your approval.'

'If I thought you were even the tiniest bit seri—' She bit off the word, but still it hung in the air for all to hear. Everyone knew Steve Anderson didn't do long-term. 'Annie. Are you okay?'

Anneliese summoned some semblance of a smile for her friend. 'I'm fine,' she lied, reading the distress on her face. 'I can't talk now, Cindy. I'll ring you. Later. I have a taxi waiting.'

All Anneliese wanted to do was go home and *not* think about the sight of Steve with bed-spiked hair, unshaven jaw tracksuit pants low on his hips and how she'd gone to sleep with her head against his chest...

He didn't want her. He didn't want the baby. She picked up her belongings, which she'd set on the sofa, and headed for the kitchen.

But she'd taken three steps into the room before he said, 'Stop.' One hand closed around her arm while his other slammed the door shut behind him, giving them privacy.

Then he turned her around, stood so close all she could see was a sudden ruthlessness in the intense brown of his irises.

She closed her own eyes to block them out, but other senses tuned in. Heat radiated from his bare chest and scorched her face. His skin still smelled warm and masculine and intimately familiar and she wanted to lean in and rest her cheek there.

How stupid was that?

When he could obviously see she wasn't going to look at him, he loosened his grip, allowing her to move away. Her spine ram-rod straight, she walked to the back door.

'We're going to discuss this.'

She'd never heard such bleakness in his voice before. 'Yes. But not now.' She did look at him then, from the safety of distance. 'Caitlyn did this to you. She made you the cynical commitment-avoider that you are.'

At the mention of his ex-lover's name it was as if a shutter had closed over his gaze, rendering his eyes obsidian and impenetrable. His eyebrows lowered and his jaw clenched. His fingers tightened at his sides.

She'd only seen that closed expression in his eyes once before. At the top of the Q1 when she'd asked him about children. She already knew—the moment she'd mentioned Caitlyn's name she knew—but she had to ask, 'Did you love her?

When he didn't answer, she shook her head. 'Why are you still letting her poison stop you from living your life?'

* * *

Sitting alone on the thirty-fifth floor in Angel-Shield Security System's office didn't give Steve the peace he desperately needed to search his heart for answers. Even the stunning water-colour reflections in the River Yarra below and spears of light from the Eureka Tower visible through the floor-to-ceiling windows failed to impress.

His shoes made no sound as he crossed the carpeted floor to the small living suite—kitchenette, bathroom, bedroom—adjoining his office where he sometimes stayed overnight if he worked late.

Or entertained his lovers.

He walked to the bedroom and stared sightlessly through the window. He hated Caitlyn for ruining his perception of marriage and kids, but she wasn't responsible for his life. He was. *Que sera sera. Life's what you make of it.* Hadn't he told Anneliese that not so long ago?

She was having his baby. The knowledge wrenched at his heart, swept through his veins in a shining river of hope. They were going to be parents. Life had given him another chance.

He picked up his phone and called Anneliese.

'Hello.'

Her voice sounded like music to his ears. He sank to the side of the bed and closed his eyes to hear her better. To imagine she was sitting in the crook of his arm, her hair against his chest, the scent of her shampoo filling his nose...

'Is anyone there?'

'Annie.' He cleared the huskiness from his throat.

'Steve.' Cool. Sad. Unapproachable.

He waited, his pulse beating in his ears, and replayed the last time they'd seen each other this morning. And waited. Finally he said, 'We need to talk. I'm coming over.'

'I'm not home so there's no point.'

'Where are you?' The demand spilled from his lips before he could halt it.

'Safe. Alone.'

And he had to be satisfied with that? Like hell. Anger and frustration rivalled for supremacy. 'You don't run away from your problems. You stick around and fix them. Which means we need to talk.'

'As you say—my *problem*, I'll fix it.'

'That's not what I meant and you know it.' A pause while he counted the lonely beat of his heart. One, two, three…

'I know it's not,' she said finally and he heard tired resignation in her voice. 'But not tonight, Steve.'

She'd disconnected before he could tell her…what? He shook his head in frustration. Before he laid his scarred heart at her feet and told her how he really felt?

Tossing the phone on the bed, he gazed at the ceiling. He'd waited years to find the love he'd searched for but never found. A real love. An honest, open love.

Anneliese.

He couldn't lose her. He *wouldn't* lose her.

Ten minutes later he picked up the phone again and began to make some enquiries.

CHAPTER SEVENTEEN

ANNELIESE had taken the opportunity while her dad was recovering in care to stay at Dreamscape, their family holiday home near Dromana, where she could still visit him daily and indulge in the solitude it offered on its huge open block of land edged by gum-trees.

This morning she was researching pregnancy on the Internet. Anneliese paused and stretched. Her mind refused to ignore Steve and images of what they'd shared. She knew he'd never disown the baby, but she didn't want his support showing up as a credit on her bank account every month. She wanted his support in person. She wanted to see him hold his own child.

She wanted him to look at her over that child's head with love in his eyes. For both of them.

Was that an impossible dream?

She hadn't seen or heard from him for two days.

This baby could heal his past hurts if he was only willing to open his heart and let it, but he'd locked that part of himself away and Anneliese had no idea where to find the key.

A detailed picture of her baby's current stage of development popped up on the screen. Her hand curved over her still-flat belly. She would protect this life with everything she had. It was hers, and at this time hers alone—and nothing would ever be as precious. She thought of her mother—both mothers—and understood, more deeply now, how much they'd loved her.

The landline phone rang and she picked up.

'Annie.'

'Steve.' Her heart's rhythm increased. 'How did you know where I was?'

'I went to see your father this morning. He told me where you are. I'm waiting outside.'

Here? Now? She clutched at the old jumper she wore. Her hair was a mess and she had no make-up on to hide the dark circles beneath her eyes.

'Let me in, Annie,' he said with a quiet firmness she'd never heard before.

Did he mean let him into the house or into her life? She didn't know, but she suspected the former. She sighed, 'Okay,' and, resigned now, she hung up the phone and walked to the front door. It was time to talk.

She pulled the door open and looked straight into his familiar brown eyes and remembered other times when she'd looked into them. In laughter, in passion. In love. It didn't make her feel better to see that he looked as sleep-deprived as she.

Steve took a moment to absorb the picture before him. He'd never seen Anneliese looking this way—casual bordering on dishevelled in an old worn jumper and black tracksuit pants, her hair hidden behind a wide fabric band, her skin pale and clear.

It made her look less remote, more real somehow, and thoroughly adorable.

He shifted his shoulders inside his caramel suede jacket and pastel blue and white checked shirt. His Adam's apple bobbed once behind his perfectly knotted blue tie as he attempted to swallow over a dry throat. The day was cool and blustery but a line of sweat was breaking out down his back. Because if this didn't work…

He saw her glance at his neat attire as she said, 'Come in.'

Instead, he went with impulse and pressed a kiss on that unpainted mouth. *Home.* 'I've missed you,' he murmured before drawing back again.

'It's only been two days.'

He could see the questions behind her eyes as she lifted her hands to straighten his tie and smooth her hands over his jacket. She turned and led him to the sofa in a casually furnished living room but he remained standing, keeping his nervous hands out of sight and clasped behind his back.

'You want to know about Caitlyn.'

Anneliese shook her head. 'Cindy told me everything. No need to open it all up again.'

He nodded once, let out a slow breath and stood silent a moment, locked in memories she could have no part in. 'I thought I could shut off my heart, play the field, live on that safe, even plane where there are no risks. And no rewards.

'But you…' He looked at her, his eyes brimming with emotion that sprang from his heart. 'You were always there in the background, reminding me that there was more to life than playing safe and that if I wanted to take a chance, maybe, just maybe, there was a prize at the end.

'Then there was that moment at your twenty-first birthday party.'

A smile flickered around her eyes. 'I was so infatuated with you it robbed me of coherent thought. I had to protect myself, so I was rude to you. I shouldn't have been.'

'I didn't want to taste your rejection again, yet you were like a drug, a craving I couldn't seem to rid myself of. And there you were turning up at my house, cluttering my thoughts too often for my peace of mind.'

He crouched in front of her, knowing he was laying his heart on the line. 'There are no guarantees in life, but I'm ready to take a chance, Annie, and I want you to take it with me. You and our baby.'

Her eyes brimmed with moisture. 'Oh...'

'We'll have to live together because I intend being a part of my child's life, too.'

Anneliese's hopes plummeted. *Live together.* The words hit her with a cold dose of reality. She knew lots of people in de facto relationships but that wasn't what she wanted for her or her baby. She thought of Abby's childhood, which very nearly could have been hers. A child deserved the very best its parents could provide, which meant living together in a *committed* relationship.

Live together, de facto, take a chance—they all smacked of commitment-avoidance and everything inside her splintered into a thousand pieces. She'd be better off on her own than facing possible heartbreak down the track. She hugged her arms around her middle. 'That won't work for me. Living together.'

He nodded, as if he'd expected her refusal, pulled out his mobile and punched in a number. 'I didn't think it would. Come with me.' Grabbing her hand, he led her out the front door, then around to the back of the house. The large allotment stretched out before them.

'What are we doing here?' She heard nothing, saw no one. Nothing but the salt wind blowing up from Port Phillip Bay tangling in her hair and a helicopter in the distance.

But even as she watched, it drew closer until it hovered overhead.

The down-draught tugged at her clothes, the throb of its rotors reverberated in her ears. She shielded her eyes and saw the door slide open and something pink tumbled out, fluttering down to earth. Rose petals.

Then something heavier. She squinted into the distance. Bootees? Thousands of them swirling as they fell softly to the ground in a rainbow of pastels. She saw a box attached to a foil balloon land on the ground a few metres away. Then the chopper rose and veered away over the bay and the scene returned to its usual tranquillity.

Except there was nothing tranquil about the way her heart throbbed, or the air between them, as he took her hand and walked with her over the petal carpet. She wanted to laugh. She wanted to cry. 'What does this mean?'

He let her go to pick up a few pairs of bootees scattered at his feet and held up a pink pair. 'A girl?' Then held out blue. 'A boy? Or twins?' he said, holding them both up.

He walked over to retrieve the foil balloon and the box, then she watched him walk back to her while her heart performed a crazy dance in her chest.

'We'll live here,' he said, holding the box in his hands. 'It's not too far from town, a few minutes from the beach. Great for kids. We can—'

She shook her head. 'This is my parents' holiday house. I'm only here until I find something of my own, then I'm leaving.'

'Well, I'm not leaving. I'm staying right here. With you.'

She shook her head. 'You didn't listen.'

'Open the box, princess.'

With fingers that weren't quite steady, she pried it open and pulled out a carefully rolled official-looking document. She frowned, then looked up at him. 'It's the title for Dreamscape.'

He nodded. 'I bought Dreamscape from your father. Last week. The paperwork still needs to be finalised with your signature added to mine.'

'*My* signature?' She seemed to be only capable of parroting his words back at him. Her throat was dry, her heart was an iron ball trying to pound its way out of her chest.

'It's in joint names. Yours and mine. This is our house, Annie.'

She felt as if she were being swept out to sea. 'We haven't discussed this. Making plans to live together to raise our child—'

'I didn't know about the baby when I made the offer for the house.' He flexed and curled his fingers, tension once again in every joint of his body as he looked past her, out to the clouds gathering over the sea. 'I bought it because I want you to marry me. Because I love you.'

Everything inside Anneliese stilled. She didn't take her eyes off him as she committed this moment to memory. Everything. From the tiny creases around his unsmiling mouth, to the way the wind tossed his hair, the fragrance of his aftershave.

'I've just come from seeing your father,' he continued, still looking out to sea. 'I asked him for permission to marry his daughter. He said yes.' Then he turned to her and she saw his hope and his fear in the depths of his dark eyes. 'What do *you* say, Annie?'

Her hands crept up to her chin. 'Oh, Steve...' she said softly, scarcely believing a man like Steve would do it all so *right*. 'You asked my father's permission?'

'I know you'd want everything traditional.' He reached to the inside pocket of his jacket and pulled out a pink and white striped oval box with a ribbon on top and lifted the lid.

Anneliese blinked at the ring nestled on white velvet. A ruby the size of her little fingernail flanked on either side by a pink diamond and set on a delicate gold band.

He lifted it with thumb and forefinger, held it between them and cleared his throat. 'Will you marry me, Anneliese Duffield?'

To her surprise, and no doubt Steve's, she burst into tears. 'I don't know what to say,' she sobbed, leaning her spinning head against the soft suede of his jacket and the solid comfort of his body.

His arms enfolded her as she pressed herself closer. 'I was hoping for a more decisive answer.' His voice rumbled like ridged velvet against her ear.

'I love you, too, Steve,' she sniffled. 'Hormones are up the creek. Of course the answer's yes.'

His hold tightened and for a moment they just stood there while the spring-scented wind eddied around them. Then he gently set her away and slipped the ring onto her finger.

A few weeks ago she'd been lost. Adrift. Alone.

And now she had a sister and a baby coming *and* she had Steve Anderson. No longer eligible for playboy of the year. She accepted the tissue Steve miraculously produced from his pocket as if he'd known she'd need one about now. As if he knew her that well.

His hand rested on their unborn child, warm, firm, protective. '*Que sera sera,* Annie. What we make of this marriage is up to both of us.'

'And we can make it work. Together. I still want to study, part-time, if I can. I've wanted to do it for so long.'

She felt his smile as he pressed a kiss on her mouth. 'That's fine. We'll work around it.'

'And you intend to travel one hour every day to your office?'

'I can work anywhere. We can look for something closer to the city or uni later, but Dreamscape will always be here. A place to relax...' his hand journeyed down the front of her thighs till it curled around the hem of her jumper '...or whatever we want to do...'

He swung her into his arms and carried her inside. Somehow they made it to the bedroom before succumbing to their long-awaited passion.

Hours later Anneliese woke to the sensation of someone

stroking her arm. Steve was sitting on the side of the bed, watching her. Late afternoon light flooded the bedroom with a bruised glow just as the first drops of rain hit the roof. She saw a plate of dry biscuits and jellybeans and a pot of tea on a tray in the middle of the bed. 'How did you know I'd need that?' she murmured, rolling over and choosing a red jellybean.

'I commandeered your laptop. Read up on some hints. I also made a list of venues available for weddings.'

She selected a green jellybean and popped it into his mouth. 'Big venues?'

'As big as you want.' He chewed and smiled, his love for her and their unborn baby shining in his eyes. 'We're good for each other.'

On that point she agreed, but she hooked a hand in the front of the T-shirt he'd changed into and pulled his face down to hers. 'Show me again, how good.'

'With pleasure, princess.'

POSH DOCS

Dedicated, daring and devastatingly handsome—these doctors are guaranteed to raise your temperature!

The new collection by your favorite authors, available in May 2009:

Billionaire Doctor, Ordinary Nurse #53
by CAROL MARINELLI

Claimed by the Desert Prince #54
by MEREDITH WEBBER

The Millionaire Boss's Reluctant Mistress #55
by KATE HARDY

The Royal Doctor's Bride #56
by JESSICA MATTHEWS

Life is a game of power and pleasure.
And these men play to win!

THE RUTHLESS BILLIONAIRE'S VIRGIN
by *Susan Stephens*

Rescued by the elusive, scarred billionaire
Ethan Alexander, Savannah glimpses the
magnificence beneath the flaws and gives
Ethan's darkened heart the salvation only
an innocent in his bed can bring....

Book #2822

Available May 2009

Eight volumes in all to collect!

NIGHTS *of* PASSION

One night is never enough!

*These guys know what they want
and how they're going to get it!*

UNTAMED BILLIONAIRE, UNDRESSED VIRGIN

by Anna Cleary

Inexperienced Sophy has fallen for dark and
dangerous Connor O'Brien. Though the bad boy
has vowed never to commit, after taking Sophy's
innocence is he still able to walk away?

Book #2826

Available May 2009

Don't miss any of these hot stories, where sparky
romance and sizzling passion are guaranteed!

www.eHarlequin.com

HP12826

REQUEST YOUR FREE BOOKS!

HARLEQUIN *Presents*®

2 FREE NOVELS
PLUS 2
FREE GIFTS!

PASSION GUARANTEED SEDUCTION